# SQUEALER

Gripping detective fiction with a great twist

# SADIE NORMAN

THE BOOK FOLKS

Published by The Book Folks

London, 2024

© Sadie Norman

This book is a work of fiction. Names, characters, businesses, organizations, places and events are either the product of the author's imagination or are used fictitiously. Any resemblance to actual persons, living or dead, events or locales is entirely coincidental. The spelling is British English.

All rights reserved. No part of this publication may be reproduced, stored in retrieval system, copied in any form or by any means, electronic, mechanical, photocopying, recording or otherwise transmitted without written permission from the publisher.

The right of Sadie Norman to be identified as the author of this work has been asserted in accordance with the Copyright, Designs and Patents Act, 1988.

ISBN 978-1-80462-238-4

www.thebookfolks.com

*SQUEALER is the second book in a series of standalone mysteries by Sadie Norman. Look out for the first, CATFISH.*

# Prologue

It was all for show.

The jovial smile, the well-fitted clothes, the sparkling jewellery. The kind words and the false compliments.

"Oh, Yvonne, you sing like an angel!"

Bullshit. Every bit of it. It was all an act, curated to project the image of perfection, and Yvonne knew that. In fact, now she'd seen the truth, she couldn't unsee it. Now she saw every deception, every tiny flaw and every crack in the perfect demeanour. It was just a facade, carefully designed to hide the truth. They were a monster. Yvonne knew monsters. She knew how well they hid their true selves from the outside world.

The trick they used was perception. Dress a devil in an expensive suit, behind the wheel of a new-reg 4x4, with a pair of designer sunglasses, and most people would see the riches first. They'd be dazzled by them; it would take them longer to see the monster hiding beneath it all. And when the monster did strike, it'd be too late for them to protect themselves. Yvonne had fallen in love with a monster, so she knew one when she saw one, even in disguise.

And right now, she was looking at a monster.

Somehow, she managed to get through the night without confronting the monster, and she returned home to an empty, darkened house. It had only just started feeling whole again after the last monster left. But it was home, and it would always be a sanctuary to her and a trophy to what she had overcome. She kind of fancied herself as a muse; maybe she could inspire others in some way to defeat their monsters. The church might not have liked her idea of a therapy group, but Yvonne wasn't ready to give up on it yet. There was plenty of people out there who needed help.

Or she could look into being a support worker, that would be really rewarding. And it might pay better than her cleaning job and the other odd bits she picked up.

She settled at the kitchen table with her nightly cup of decaf tea, trying to get the image of the monster's dishonest smile out of her mind, when she heard a knock at the door. She considered herself before answering, because it was late now, but it was sure to be important if someone wanted her at this time.

And just when she thought she'd finished with one monster for the night, she found herself face to face with another.

## Chapter One

Although I would never admit it to anyone in real life, I was one of those people who skipped to the last pages of a book, to find out the ending first before the beginning. The unknown gnawed at me, grating steadily until I could no longer resist the urge to find out. Because if I had known that this call would come through this morning, when the ground was damp and mushy, I would have worn some more sensible shoes for my expedition through the pine woodland to view some human remains.

The sandy soil caved under my feet like walking on a beach, but I pressed on because I wasn't going to let this morning be the morning that I messed things up. I had waited patiently for my colleagues to trust me enough to let me go out on a call on my own, my first one as a fully fledged member of the Serious Crimes team, and I wasn't going to fuck it up. Soggy, sandy shoes be damned, I was going to prove my worth.

As the trees loomed around me, their needles hiding the sky and any prying eyes above, I revelled in the peacefulness. It was like there wasn't another soul for a thousand miles. I was nearing the edge of the woods, where they met the harvested farmland to the east, and now I could see the short golden plain at the end of the track I followed. I reviewed what little info I had about the call and imagined what the poor person I was meeting felt. From the minimal details I had, a tractor driver had stumbled across remains whilst ploughing his field. I could imagine his surprise as the plough crunched over a heavy rock – at least he hoped it was a heavy rock. But then the plough mostly pushed them out of the way, and the soil was far too sandy round here to have many boulders hidden in it.

Maybe he thought he'd hit an animal. Or a fallen branch. I bet he huffed as he stopped the tractor, hopped out of the cab and took a look.

Bones. Most likely human.

Which was why it was so strange that my colleagues had given me this job on my own. In the three short months since I had joined their team, Detective Inspector Chris Hamill and Detective Sergeant Jay Fitzgerald hadn't trusted me enough to lead an interview on my own, let alone attend a call-out. Finding bones usually required a larger turnout than one detective. There was something else going on, I was sure of it.

As I neared the end of the trail, the pine trees thinning and daylight breaching the canopy in patchy shafts from above, my mobile phone rang. I was surprised to have signal this far into the West Norfolk wilderness and a glance at the screen showed me it was one of the few people whose number I had now bothered to save – *DCI Aaron Burns*.

"Detective Constable McArthur, where are you?" he asked, although his tone was conversational rather than abrupt, which led me to believe that he was alone in his office.

"Somewhere deep in the Shouldham Woods," I replied, feeling a smile tug at my lips. I gazed around at the trees, as though they might help me explain where I was. All they offered was a rustle as an early autumn breeze whistled through above.

"The Sincks or the Warren?"

"The second one, the Warren."

Aaron hummed knowingly. Yet another reminder that to him, I was an outsider, not having been born and raised in the West Norfolk countryside like he was. Just like how I sometimes still felt like an outsider to my colleagues, eagerly waiting to earn my place.

"What are you doing out there?"

"We had a call-out to a farm on the east side of the woodland. Human remains have been found by a farmer ploughing his field." It surprised me that he didn't already know this. Something as exciting as human remains usually warranted informing the Detective Chief Inspector; the big boss.

"Ah," said Aaron, sounding even more knowing now. In fact, he had a similar tone to Chris and Jay when they first heard about the job.

"What?" I asked, starting to feel a self-conscious flush creep up my neck. Everyone was so blasé about a potential new case. I mean, bones in a field. This wasn't a simple crime. This was a suspicious death at the least, a full-blown murder at worst.

But Aaron sniggered down the line. "Nothing."

"What is it?"

He drew in a breath. "Well, as Detective Chief Inspector and Station Lead of King's Lynn Police, I do not condone hazing in any form. But this is one of those cases that the rookie always gets sent to, like a rite of passage for Serious Crimes. It's just a waste of time otherwise."

"Human remains are just a waste of time?" Had I somehow travelled to an alternate dimension, where policing standards were so lax that dead bodies were just an inconvenience?

"You'll see when you get there, it's a straightforward one. Just don't Crazy-McArthur it up."

"Is my nickname a verb now?"

"Always has been. Anyway, I wasn't calling you for that, Anna."

"Then why were you calling?"

I reached the end of the trail, the towering pines giving way to a lush scenery of open fields, with green hedgerows fading to orange and red as autumn took over summer. Ahead of me, a small blue tractor towing a matching plough sat in the field, having only ploughed one furrow around the edge. The tractor driver, a young lad with a flat cap, was waiting beside the machine, talking to an older lady dressed in high wellington boots caked in mud.

I paused at the edge of the woods. Compared to the bright autumnal morning ahead, the woods were chilling and devoid of warmth. The canopy trapped the darkness in. Deep inside, nothing penetrated their concealed fortress, not birdsong nor sunlight. It was like stepping into another time.

"Have you got plans for tonight?" Aaron asked.

I rolled my eyes. I never had plans and I told him so.

"Good," he said. "Tea at my place?"

"How about at mine?" I was starting to miss my own bed.

"Okay. I should get off about six. I'll cook."

"You always cook," I complained.

"That's because you're terrible at it," he replied easily. I could hear the grin in his voice, a rare smile that not many people saw from him.

"All right, but you might have to wait outside for me. I don't know when I'll get off. Depends on what this case turns into."

I heard stifled laughter down the line. Whenever I found out what was really going on with this call-out, I would plan my revenge for being the butt of some unknown joke.

"You won't be late," he said cryptically.

"Maybe I should get you your own key," I said as I entered the field, my feet sinking even further into the ground on the freshly furrowed soil. "That way we don't need to have this conversation every time we want to see each other after work."

"Um."

Oh shit. That was completely the wrong thing to say.

"Um," he said again. "I better go. Let me know how you get on with the caveman bones."

And with that, the line went dead.

I didn't know what to label my new relationship with Aaron as, but one of the best words to describe it was 'tentative'. We kept things under wraps for a range of reasons. We were colleagues. We also had the misfortune of working in one of the most gossip-ridden police stations in the whole country. How we'd managed to keep things QT for three whole months was a miracle.

And finally, Aaron was the most commitment-phobic person I had ever met. One push in the wrong direction and it would all be over.

I sucked in a deep breath of air, tinged with fertiliser and diesel from the tractor. Why did I even say that?

With the frustration still smarting, I released my burning lungs and turned to the task at hand. The young farmer and older woman were watching with me with curious looks, trying hard not to look like they were too interested. I waded my way over to them, almost tripping over the deep furrows as I went.

"You're new," said the older woman, just as I opened my mouth to introduce myself.

"I, um…" What did that even mean? "I'm Detective Constable Anna McArthur, with King's Lynn police. Someone called about some suspected human remains." I flashed my warrant card from my back pocket but neither looked interested.

"Not 'suspected'," replied the woman, scratching at her forehead with muddy hands, "they're definitely human."

She pointed to the ground by the edge of the tractor plough, where one large bone, possibly a femur, was sticking out of the mud.

"Right." I looked from one to the other, bewildered. "And how do you know that?"

The woman laughed to herself and looked to the young farmer. "I told you they'd send a newbie, didn't I? They always do."

"Who are you?" I asked. The words came out far ruder than I intended, but I was still mad at myself for possibly botching things with Aaron. I wasn't in the mood for cryptic games now.

"Zoe Nicholls, professor of Forensic Archaeology at UEA."

Ah. That explained a little.

"I always get called out when anything is found here," she continued, giving the young man a nod. "This might be young Will's first time uncovering something here, but it's certainly not mine. I've spent years digging these woods."

"So, this bone is…"

Zoe narrowed her eyes at the dull grey object. It was too thick to be a stick, and the end looked splintered. Thinly veiled excitement grew across her face.

"Medieval," she said. "At a guess. Obviously, I'd need to take it back to my lab for carbon-dating."

"Take it," grunted the young farmer. "The old man will have a fit if I don't get this field ploughed today."

"Woah, wait a moment." I held my hands up. This was my first solo outing, potentially my first case alone. I couldn't just let it go like that, and to some random member of the public too. "We need to establish whether a crime has been committed here."

"Is running over an ancient bone with a tractor a crime?" Zoe asked.

"Well, no."

"Then there's no crime here."

"That's not for you to decide," I said, gritting my teeth.

Zoe folded her arms and smiled to herself again. "All right. I'll go through the investigative motions for you, I cancelled my morning lecture anyway. Tell me though, which one of them sent you here?"

I frowned back at her. This woman was testing my patience. "Which who?"

"Which officer?" she said. "I bet it was DI Hamill, he's a bugger for sending the new recruits to these calls."

"Er… actually it was DS Jay Fitzgerald."

I could still hear Jay's delighted voice as I walked into the office that morning, telling me there had been a call I had to attend to right away. He'd scribbled the details and address down for me before practically pushing me back out the door, promising me that this was a case I could deal with myself. Chris Hamill, although present in the room, hadn't said a word the whole time, but that wasn't unusual for Chris.

"Oh, that git," Zoe said fondly. "I remember when he was first sent out here, all young and fresh-faced. It was a jawbone that time."

The farmer wrinkled his nose as Zoe stared wistfully at the femur, more like a dog than a professor.

"Hang on," I said. "Is this a regular occurrence? Finding human remains out here near the woods?"

And as if my frustration wasn't evident enough, both Zoe and Will the farmer nodded obviously and shared a look of pity.

"This whole area is renowned for its rich archaeological finds," said Zoe. "From Neolithic to Roman occupation to medieval, there's always been settlements in Shouldham and the surrounding woodland. Some of the finds are amazing. One young lad working in the fields in the fifties found an almost entire skeleton. It's in Norwich museum now."

"That's…" I searched for an appropriate word, one that wasn't insulting. "Fascinating," I settled on. "But how can we be sure that is the case with this bone?"

I motioned to the femur, sticking out of the ground like a sad tree root, cut off from its body. I'd dealt with plenty of dead bodies over my several years on the police force, but I didn't have enough experience to say for certain that this bone belonged to an ancient human.

"Ah well, that's the best bit." Zoe bopped down to her haunches and poked at the bone with a pen from her pocket. "See the rippling in the top layer and the way it's splintered so easily? Modern man has stronger bones, we drink far more calcium than our ancestors. And metal detectors found some medieval coins on this very field a few years ago. This was probably a burial site."

Well, she sounded convincing at the very least. But it still rankled that this woman expected me to just take her word for it. My presence here was merely a formality, given that I couldn't be any help at all other than to write up the paperwork and close the case when back at the nick.

"And the rest of the bones?"

Zoe waved her arms around here. "They'll be here somewhere. Another dry summer and sudden rainfall, and a few more might make it to the surface."

"Can I get on now?" Will the farmer asked, wrinkling his nose again. "I can do the other side and leave this side for later."

"Yes, please," Zoe jumped in before I could answer. "I'll get my kit and extract it."

The two sprang into action before I was even able to think of a reply. I thought about stamping my feet, about telling the two of them in no uncertain terms that this was a crime scene until I said it wasn't, and that they should listen to the authority on the matter – me. But before I had a chance to line up my protest, my mobile phone rang again, and I answered it to find my dear colleague Jay on the line.

"Come on," he said, speaking before I could. "We need you back here, another call's come in."

"I'm still dealing with the first call," I replied stiffly.

"Still?" he said. "What did Zoe say? It'll be medieval, it always is out there. Let Zoe finish it up and take the bones to her lab."

"You knew this was an archaeological find?" If looks could kill, I was wondering how much mine could have hurt Jay in that moment. I felt like the time my dad sent me into his garage to find a left-handed hammer in his toolbox.

He sniggered back, quickly and wisely turning it into a cough as he cleared his throat. "Yeah. That's why I called Zoe out there too."

"Then why did you send me?"

"Because we have to attend, even if it's some ancient pig farmer who fell off his wagon one day or succumbed to the plague or whatever. It's a waste of time, Zoe knows what she's doing. Now hurry up. I'll send you the address to go to," he said, then hung up.

Once again, I took a deep breath, ignoring the smell of the field and the mutterings of Will and Zoe as they carried on.

So, I still had a lot to prove to Chris and Jay, another case to attend, and a tentative new relationship to smooth over with Aaron. This day was off to a great start.

## Chapter Two

When the address came through from Jay, I made my excuses to Zoe and Will, the young farmer, and headed off on a comfortingly familiar route back to the small town of Downham Market. The address was barely half a mile from my own home in the centre of town, where I lived down a quiet side street in a converted shop. This journey took me through to a road near the train station lined with pretty cottages and post-war terraced houses, called Nelson Avenue. At the end of the street, a church stood nestled in between two giant oak trees. It wasn't the main church in town – that was St Edmund's, which stood on a hill by the traffic lights, quite notable and obvious since hills were a rare sight in West Norfolk. This one was St Mary's Church, a rather small stone structure with a bell tower obscured by the overhanging trees. In their shadows was a small car park and community centre. Today, the church and community centre lay forlorn compared to the commotion half a street away, where a host of police cars blocked the avenue.

I parked my car as close as I could get and walked the last stretch on the leaf-strewn pavements, approaching the police cordon at the top of the road. A group of onlookers was starting to form, taking pictures of the police, although the forensics van had been cleverly parked lengthways in the street and covered up most of the activity. Two officers stood guard at the scene cordon, eyeing the crowd with indifference, and they waved me through as I approached.

"Morning, Anna," my old shift colleague Pres greeted me. He stood with Frenchy at the cordon line, speaking to me with his back to the onlookers.

"Morning, Pres. Bit of an early one," I replied. I certainly didn't miss my uniformed days spent manning a flimsy line of tape and fielding questions from the nosy public.

"You can say that again. I should have got off shift an hour ago."

Frenchy looked even more annoyed at the overtime than Pres.

"Who was the first responder?" I asked them both.

Pres pointed to himself. "Muggins here. Had a call come from the control room and I was the closest. The victim's neighbours called it in, they were concerned they hadn't seen the victim at church the day before. They popped round and used a spare key to enter, and found the carnage inside."

"Is it that bad?" I asked.

Pres wrinkled his nose and nodded. I liked Pres, short for Preston; he was one of the old colleagues from my time in uniform that I missed working with the most. Always friendly and up for a laugh, he had made sergeant about six months ago. As the senior ranking officer on site, he was stuck doing unwanted overtime until someone more senior came along. The senior officers we were waiting for were Chris and Jay; my colleagues and supervisors in the Serious Crimes team.

I scanned the street but there was no sign of them yet. "I'm going to check out the scene," I said.

"Go for it." Pres held up the scene tape for me to duck underneath. "It's the middle terrace house, closest to the church."

I made my way over. There were three cottages joined together; the two either side had been extended over the years, but the one in the middle was still tiny and untouched by modernisation. There was barely enough room to park the small white Fiat 500 in the driveway out front, and the scene-of-crime officers were having to squeeze past to get to the front door. The property was just a small two-up, two-down with a little plaque on the garden wall that read *2 Churchside Cottages*. It looked even cosier than my flat.

Donning gloves and shoe covers, I headed inside the cramped premises. This house wasn't designed for more than one person to live in, certainly not ten police officers all trying to do their jobs. A few moved out of the way so I could get a closer look at the property; I could tell it was tidy and clean. An undertone of lavender wafted from a diffuser by the front door, soon overpowered by the sharp stench of blood. Narrow stairs were to the left and a living room to the right. At the end of the hallway was the kitchen, the source of the buzzing activity and intrusive smell. I moved slowly through the house, taking it all in and being careful not to touch anything. A morbid excitement grew inside me; this was a case to get stuck into. A proper one. I had learned in recent months that I needed work to fuel my recovery from an all-consuming slump. I needed to be busy and distracted, and solving murders was the most distracting activity I knew.

The victim lay just inside the internal kitchen door. The body was partially hidden by a small kitchen table, shoved up against the far wall. The cause of the stench was unmissable. Blood, congealed and crimson, covered the kitchen floor and splattered two of the walls like a bad piece of art. There couldn't have been a drop left in the body. The sheer amount of it was unlike anything I had seen before. Everything shined unnaturally under the coating of forbidden paint.

The body itself lay in an unnatural position; a woman, probably in her mid-fifties – it was quite hard to tell. Her legs were flayed out and one arm was pinned underneath her body. The smell of decomposition wasn't bad; she hadn't been dead long. I felt a pang of guilt and sadness for the woman, laying mangled in her own home in a pool of her own blood.

I felt a presence behind my shoulder and glanced around. It was my teammate, Detective Sergeant Jay Fitzgerald.

"Yvonne Garrington," he said to me quietly, reading from his notebook as if pressing his nose against the pages might help with the smell. "Fifty-four, divorced and lived alone. Her next-door neighbours found her this morning after they grew worried and let themselves in using the spare back door key they had."

"I have never seen so much blood." I mumbled the words, not wanting to look like an amateur in front of everyone. But still, this was beyond a normal crime scene. This was like an over-the-top horror movie. A true bloodbath.

Jay hummed in agreement, his voice wavering. "Me neither. Must have severed a main artery. Looks like her throat has been slashed."

How he could tell that from the sheer amount of blood covering everything, including the body, I didn't know.

"That's a brutal way of killing someone," I said. "Have the SOCOs found a weapon yet?"

Jay flicked to another page of his notebook, practically eating the pages. "Kitchen knife, it's in the sink. It's been cleaned with bleach."

There were signs of a scuffle having occurred in the kitchen under all the blood – a plate knocked from the dining table; a vase of flowers scattered over the floor. A pair of shattered glasses lay next to her, alongside the smashed pieces of what was once a mug. Any liquid it might have held was now lost to the puddle of blood.

"No footprints," I observed, which seemed quite an accomplishment with the amount of blood. "Plenty of signs of a struggle though. Maybe there is…"

I heard footsteps and turned to see Jay had disappeared, heading straight back out the front door. I followed him to the front, where our team leader, Detective Inspector Chris Hamill, had also arrived and was leaning against the low brick wall separating the victim's driveway from her neighbour's front garden.

"Is it that bad?" he asked Jay as he approached, the older man's eyes widening at the younger's face.

Jay nodded weakly. He looked a little peaky, his usually tanned skin washed out in the morning light. He sagged against the garden wall like gravity had doubled for him, for once not caring that he might get his trendy, expensive jacket dirty.

"It's not pleasant," he said. "I wish I had a steel stomach like Anna here does."

I shrugged, feeling a little bad. The smell was in my nose, but my guts were fine and unaffected by the scene. "It's definitely one of the worst I've seen," I said, just to make him feel better. "Where should we start?"

"I want to take a good look around the property," Chris said, straight to business, as usual. He rubbed a hand over his chin as he thought, bristling his two-day-old grey stubble. "Jay, you can take upstairs if your stomach can handle it. Anna, talk to the neighbours who found the victim and get their statements."

I nodded at my orders, keen to get started; so keen, in fact, that I was willing to overlook the waste of time they'd sent me on earlier that morning. This was not a formality, this was a murder, and after seeing the carnage, I was ready to get stuck in and to find the person responsible for causing such destruction to life. Someone brutally killed Yvonne Garrington, and it was up to us to find them.

\* \* \*

Yvonne's terraced house was by far the smallest property on this road. Groups of cottages just like Yvonne's lined both sides of the street, all immaculate and well-maintained with beautiful gardens crowned by trees, their leaves turning orange and pale yellow as autumn arrived. This was a road primarily for people in early retirement, with big enough pensions for flashy new cars and enough time to cut their grass to the uniformed half inch.

The attached next-door neighbours to the right were holed up inside with a family liaison officer, who was giving them strong tea and sympathy. I found it charming how neighbourly the street seemed to be; keeping each other's keys, checking on each other. My parents had a similar relationship with their neighbours. I wondered if it was a semi-retired people thing. I barely had time to speak to my neighbours, although I usually found that was for the best.

The immediate neighbours to the left were not home and an officer was tasked with following that up.

I headed next door, walking round the old brick garden wall, and entered the home of Mr and Mrs Welles. Their kitchen was white, modern and light, a far cry from the poky home I had just come from. This one didn't smell like blood, rather there was a hint of cinnamon in the air, like someone had been baking.

"Mr and Mrs Welles," I said, sitting down opposite them. The smell made my stomach rumble, but I did my best to look as serious and official as the occasion called for.

"Please, dear, call us Robert and Sue," the woman said kindly. She smiled at me, her tight dyed-blonde hair pinching at her cheeks and crinkling her eyes, which were red from crying.

Her husband, Robert, sat with a deep, unmoving frown and a half-empty cup of coffee in front of him. "What was your name again?" he asked, eyeing me with suspicion.

"Anna McArthur," I replied, pulling out my notebook and pen. "Detective Constable Anna McArthur."

"McArthur." Robert mulled over my name. "I don't remember a McArthur."

"Oh, Robert!" Sue scolded him, with a forced chuckle. "You retired over fifteen years ago. Of course you weren't in the force the same time as this young girl."

I didn't let them see me wrinkle my nose at being called a young girl. "Were you in the force, Mr Welles?"

"Thirty years." He nodded and now I recognised that unwavering scowl as a typical policeman's stare. "Spent most of it in Traffic, I was a dog handler too though. What team are you in?"

"Serious Crimes."

"Ah. That's why you're here then. Yvonne was murdered."

Robert Welles didn't need me to confirm that for him, the sheer amount of police presence must have been a dead giveaway that his neighbour's death was certainly suspicious. People didn't tend to die with that much blood loss on their own.

"Bit young to be in CID, aren't you? Especially Serious Crimes."

"Robert!" Sue exclaimed.

I couldn't help but let out a little laugh. Young and female; according to old-school coppers like Robert Welles, I was everything a police officer shouldn't be. I rarely bothered to explain myself when faced which such outdated opinions but I decided, just this once, I'd answer Mr Welles so we could get this chat moving along.

"I've been a detective for three years; I've been on attachment with Serious Crimes for a few months now. Before that, I was in Response, but I did a few stints in neighbourhood policing. You can ask anyone outside; I'm as good an officer as any other."

Usually, younger detectives swapped teams every two years or so. It was good to rotate teams and learn new skills along the way before heading up the career ladder. It was still early days for my stint in Serious Crimes but I was determined to make it work.

"Anyway, enough about me. I'm here about Yvonne. What happened this morning?"

With another scolding look at her husband, Sue spoke. "Well, we hadn't seen Yvonne at church yesterday morning, which is strange for her. So, I decided to drop off her new dress and check she was all right. She'd asked me to take the waist in a little on my sewing machine; she's lost a lot of weight recently, you see. It was early but I knew she would be up; Yvonne is an early bird. I knocked on the back door like I always do but there was no answer. Her car was still out front and the curtains were open so I assumed she was up. I went back to the house to fetch Robert and the spare key we kept for her. I was afraid she had slipped in the bath or something. Well, then…"

"I took one look through the door and told Sue to call the police immediately," Robert concluded. "I could see blood on the floor and walls. That amount of blood splatter, I knew she wasn't alive."

"Robert!"

"Sorry, Sue…" He winced at himself. He hadn't meant to slip into police mode.

"Do you know of anyone who might have wanted to hurt Yvonne?" I asked.

"No." Sue shook her head hollowly. "Everyone loved her. She was involved a lot in the church group, running the community centre at the end of the road. She has an ex-husband but he's in Spain somewhere, they divorced about a year ago."

"Does she have any other family? Children or a partner?"

They both shook their heads. "No, not that we know of."

"When was the last time you saw her?"

"Saturday evening," Robert answered. "We had just got home from the supermarket when she set off for the community centre, for a rehearsal, I think. We waved goodnight. We thought we would see her for the Sunday service yesterday morning, but she never showed up."

"Did you see anyone arriving at Yvonne's house between Saturday night and this morning? Anyone visit, any cars parked outside?"

They both shook their heads.

"What about hearing anything? Did you hear Yvonne arrive back from her rehearsal?"

Husband and wife shared a look, and Sue offered me a sheepish smile. "No, sorry. We're not as young as we used to be. I'm in bed by nine and can sleep through a hurricane. Robert pops a sleeping pill at ten and that's him gone too."

"What about the neighbours on the other side of the terrace?" I gestured in the vague direction with my pen.

"Barry and Sue," replied Sue knowingly. "The other Sue, I mean. They've gone away. Three-week cruise around the Norway fjords and Iceland. They won't be back for another week."

Okay, so despite charmingly close neighbours, none of them were likely to have heard the carnage taking place next door.

"Did Yvonne mention she was seeing anyone?" I asked.

"Seeing someone?" Sue repeated, her face flushing to a rosy red as she hid a girlish smile.

"I mean, like, did Yvonne have any regular visitors? Any one likely to pop over, friends or otherwise?"

"No, the only visitors she ever got were from that church group," said Robert.

"Do you know the names of anyone from the church group?"

"Yes, of course. I can get you a list, it's always on the order of service." Sue jumped to her feet.

I waved her to sit back down. "Thanks, we'll sort that when we're finished talking. How about the name of Yvonne's ex-husband?"

"Keith." Sue shuffled in her seat and aimed an unsure look at her husband. "Although she didn't usually call him by his name."

"Was it not an amicable break-up?"

Sue almost laughed, but it was an uneasy sound. "Not at all. He ran off to Spain with a girl thirty years younger than him and left her to deal with the fallout. He was in debt up to his eyeballs. She normally called him a swear word, which I wouldn't care to repeat in front of such young ears."

Robert rolled his eyes at his wife. "Sue, she's a police officer. I'm sure she's heard every swear word you know and more."

"I'm sure I've been *called* every swear word you know and more," I joked.

"Oh, all right then," Sue said, "she called him a money-grabbing bastard."

I caught Robert Welles throw a glance at me. We had definitely heard worse than that.

As Sue fetched the contacts of the church down the road, I took the details down and promised to contact Robert and Sue again once we knew more of what happened to Yvonne. They were nice people; a little nosy but it was clear the unexpected death of their neighbour had shaken them this morning. They reminded me a bit of what my parents would be like in ten years' time when Dad had fully retired; nothing better to do than to be good neighbours. *Really* good neighbours.

## Chapter Three

I left Jay and Chris at the crime scene and headed back to our office at the police station on the outskirts of the next town over, King's Lynn. I didn't feel the need to go back inside Yvonne Garrington's house; there was only so much staring at blood and death I could take and I was the least-sensitive of the group – Jay looked positively green when I left. I was still a bit pissed off at them for sending me wandering through the woods that morning as well, so it was best to get back to the office before I said something I'd regret.

Both Jay and Chris insisted on talking to the church group at the community centre before heading back to the office themselves. I warned them they wouldn't get anywhere – the community centre didn't open on Mondays – but they both ignored me and went there anyway. I knew that community centre well from my days on the beat. Down a secluded, quiet residential street and overshadowed by towering oak trees, the car park was a favourite hang-out spot for some of the local youths who liked to get up to no good when the sun went down. For a few years, I made it a part of my usual rounds, popping in to see what mischief I could catch them doing. I knew the centre was closed on Mondays, and so did the youths.

Once I had settled at my desk with a strong cup of coffee, I set to work running a background check on our victim, Yvonne Garrington. I could still smell her blood, the stench clawed up my nose, bringing back images of the carnage in her kitchen. I tried to ignore it and push it far to the back of my mind where I was also ignoring Chris and Jay's cruel hazing and Aaron's relationship panic. I let the tasks consume me, disregarding all other distractions, until the office door opened.

Aaron glanced around the room, finding me alone. Tall, broad-shouldered and with a searing blue gaze, Aaron was every inch the stoic detective. His face gave nothing away of what he was thinking or feeling, and only a true master could detect what was going on inside his head. From the way he quickly averted his gaze, I guessed he was still embarrassed about earlier.

"No Chris or Jay yet?" he asked flatly.

I watched him carefully, waiting for a slip in his demeanour. Nothing. He tugged on his shirt collar absently, scratching the back of his neck where his almost-greying hair started. The very spot I'd ran my hands over that morning, whilst pulling him in for a kiss before we stepped out into the outside world, and into reality.

"No, they're still at the crime scene," I replied. "They should be back soon."

Aaron nodded once in confirmation before turning back to the door.

"Wait," I called after him. We may have been at work, but I couldn't let him go without addressing the obvious.

He paused, and glanced at me with a fleeting look.

"What I said earlier," I began.

He cut in right away. "It doesn't matter."

"Yes, it does. I didn't mean to take you by surprise, I didn't—"

"Anna," he said. In the silence, he listened carefully to the heavy clinks of footsteps on metal floating up the stairs.

"Now isn't the time," said Aaron. "We'll discuss it later."

His caution was well-founded as two seconds later, Chris and Jay burst into the office. They ignored Aaron and me as they shrugged off their coats and sat down at their desks with mild grumbles.

"I told you the community centre was shut on Mondays," I said with a smirk.

"Shut up," Jay snapped back. "Joke's on you. There's a choir concert on there tonight and we're going."

"We?" I sneered at the thought. "A concert?"

"Yeah. The church choir singing some churchy songs. What better way to get the low-down on Yvonne and this church group than to see them in action."

"I can't, I already have plans tonight," I said.

But my excuse fell on deaf ears as Jay settled down at his desk, producing two lime-green pieces of paper from his pocket and handing one over to me. "Nice try. You're coming with me. Chris is pulling the family card and I'm not going on my own."

I shared a look with Aaron – our chat was going to have to wait.

* * *

"What's up with Aaron?" Jay asked me.

The evening was drawing in and it was already twilight as we made our way across the community centre car park. There were plenty of cars already here. The church stood beside the car park, illuminated by stark white floodlights at the bottom, giving it a haunting vibe. The ghostly white tower loomed over the street like a king watching over his domain. I could hear the dull thrum of conversation from inside the community centre, a squat seventies building next to the church, which bathed the rest of the car park in a warm orange glow from the wood-panelled windows.

"What do you mean?" I asked, squashing down the spike of anxiety I felt every time someone mentioned Aaron to me.

"He's like… I dunno. Happy. He keeps smiling. It's weird."

I laughed, the only reaction I could think of. "Weird? What's wrong with him being happy?"

"Well, he's normally stressed out and a bit shouty." Jay shrugged. "But he seems so chilled and relaxed lately. Has he got a new girlfriend?"

I paused at the door to the community centre and gave Jay my best forced frown. I didn't want to be the subject of the latest gossip of the week, and I definitely didn't want to put Aaron through that.

"Probably," I answered. "He hasn't said. So, what's the plan?"

Jay shook his head. "He must have a girlfriend. He's getting some."

"Getting some?"

"Why else would he be so chilled out?"

"I'll quiz him next time I see him. What's the plan?"

Jay removed his jacket and folded it over his arms. "I guess we mingle and schmooze. Have covert conversations on the down-low, see what we can uncover. Most of these people must have known Yvonne. Just don't go Crazy-McArthuring it up again."

I was beginning to think that I would never shift the unwanted moniker, but then after our last case working together, Jay and the others had every right to call me crazy. I took a deep breath and steadied myself, promising that no matter what, I was not going to continue feeding into this unwanted reputation.

We let ourselves into the centre. The small foyer was empty but a large colourful display adorned the wall, highlighting all the events the church group ran in the centre. There were a few am-dram productions, bingo nights, craft fairs. I glanced over it, spotting a few photos with our victim in them, smiling as much as the others she was with.

Further inside, the main hall was teeming with people. It was stereotypical of middle England; almost everyone was early retirement age, white and well-dressed. The room hadn't been redecorated since it was built in the seventies.

A stage sat at the far end, obscured by musty blue curtains. Rows and rows of seats were starting to fill up.

The doors slammed closed behind us and a good ten people stopped and stared.

"I don't think covert conversations on the down-low are going to work," I mumbled to Jay.

He thrust his hands into his pockets and settled an officious scowl across his face, almost daring any of the spectators to question us. "We must have 'police' written across our foreheads," he agreed.

One of the reluctant-looking crowd approached us. It was the vicar, dressed in faded black robes and with dishevelled white hair crowning his egg-shaped head.

"Greetings, welcome," he said enthusiastically, shaking both our hands. "Our congregation welcomes all newcomers. I am Reverend Harding, but you can call me Brian. Welcome to our concert."

"Nice to meet you," Jay replied, without actually meaning it. "I am Detective Sergeant Fitzgerald; this is Detective Constable McArthur. We're here about Yvonne Garrington."

"Oh yes." The reverend paled, until his skin matched his pasty hair. "God rest her soul. Ghastly business. Please tell me you have the monster who could do such a thing behind bars."

He looked alarmed when Jay and I exchanged a look.

"The investigation is ongoing," Jay said.

Reverend Harding recovered quickly and put on a smiling face for his flock. "Well, let us help in whatever way we can. The concert is about to start, but you are welcome to enjoy some refreshments in the meantime."

"Thank you," I said genuinely and wandered off, leaving Jay to carry on talking to Reverend Harding before I got stuck with him myself.

I made my way around the hall, earning looks as I scooted between chairs. No one dared approach me, they just stared and halted their conversations as I neared. They eyed me suspiciously, as though I was the one who had killed Yvonne. For a supposedly pious group of people, not many of them were following the reverend's lead and welcoming the newbies.

On the stage at the front of the hall, the choir were faffing around, getting their sheet music ready and looking out at their audience with excited whispers. But a young lad sitting on the edge of the platform drew my attention. He watched the room without interacting with anyone, face set in a moody frown typical of a teenager – a mixture of disgust and embarrassment.

I approached and perched myself on the stage next to him. "Hi."

"Hi," he said cautiously. "You the police woman?"

"Yeah, that's me," I replied. I held out my hand to him. "My name's Anna. What's yours?"

"Jacob."

He shook my hand quickly, his palms clammy. My presence flustered him and his frown disappeared. He was young – easily the youngest person here and one of only a handful under the age of forty. I guessed about sixteen, but he was well over a foot taller than me and was starting to grow a fluffy stubble around his baby face.

"Do you know many of the people here, Jacob?" I asked, as we surveyed the room.

"Yeah, everyone," he said. "My parents are part of the church council. I've been coming here since I can remember."

"Who are your parents?"

He pointed to a middle-aged couple schmoozing across the way with pristine designer clothes and snooty expressions to match. They gave us a sidelong glance as they spoke. Jacob shared their looks; his mother had the same light-blonde hair as him and his father the same round face and angled chin.

"Who else is on the church council?"

"The reverend and that guy there, Mr Cates. George Cates. Just those four." He pointed to an elderly man in a flat cap, already sitting in the audience.

"And what does the church council do?"

Jacob shrugged and curled his top lip. "Church stuff. Look after the buildings. Put on events like this. That sort of stuff."

"Did you know Yvonne well?"

The young lad looked at me when I suddenly changed the subject, but I gave him a friendly smile. "Don't worry; you're not in any trouble. I'm just trying to find out who would have wanted to hurt her."

"She was hurt by someone?" Jacob asked with a gulp. "I heard she was dead but not that…"

"We're just enquiring," I assured him. "All unexpected deaths are investigated."

"She was the cleaner, I didn't really talk to her, but she was friendly with my parents. She was friendly with everyone. She was, you know, a nice person."

A choir member suddenly hissed across the stage at us. "Jacob, we're ready!"

Jacob stood up and gave me an apologetic look before his face settled back into his teenage scowl. "Sorry, I'm doing the curtains."

"No problem, thanks for your help."

I rejoined Jay at the back of hall as everyone else took their seats. The stage curtains rustled and the lights dimmed.

Jay leaned close to me. "Find out anything?"

"Not much," I whispered back. "But I know who we need to talk to."

\* \* \*

The concert and the choir were actually rather good. They did mostly hymns and other ecclesiastical music with the odd modern hit thrown in. When I say modern, I mean eighties classic pop and soft rock, but still, I liked eighties music as much as the next person. Who doesn't want to hear a church choir sing Duran Duran?

After thirty-five minutes, there was an intermission and drinks of wine and ale were generously passed around. As Jay and I declined a drink, not wanting to seem unprofessional, I noticed Jacob's parents standing alone across the hall. I motioned to Jay and he followed.

"Hello," I greeted them. They stiffened at my arrival, as though every breath we dared take was an intrusion. "We are—"

"We know who you are." The woman sneered at me. "We saw you talking to our son. You're the police. You're here about Yvonne."

The man took his ale-less arm and put it around his wife's shoulders.

"Sorry," he said, not seeming it at all. "We're all just so shocked about what's happened. I'm John Brandon, this is my wife, Helena."

"Nice to meet you," said Jay. He kept the friendly smile on his face, despite Helena Brandon's disparaging glare. "Did you know Yvonne well?"

"Yes, very," John Brandon answered. "We welcomed her into our group about a year ago when she took on the job of cleaner for the premises, and she's been a firm part of the family ever since. In fact, she should have been singing in this concert tonight. The show must go on, though."

I caught Jay shoot a look at me; if Yvonne was that much a part of the 'family', why not postpone the concert?

"When was the last time you saw Yvonne?" I asked.

Helena Brandon sniffed loudly, her face contorting as though a bee had stung her nose. "Saturday night, same as everyone else here. We did a final rehearsal here and then she walked home."

"Who else was here for the rehearsal?"

"Well, all the choir. There was us and Jacob, our son, and George Cates." She pointed to the front of the hall. "We stayed until last, we locked up the hall."

I glanced back at the man in a flat cap, still in his seat in the front row. Wrinkled and wiry, he was even older than the reverend. From the way he sat with his head lolling to the side, I couldn't be sure if he was asleep or not.

"And no one saw her on Sunday? Didn't you find it strange she wasn't at the Sunday church service?" I asked.

"No." Helena Brandon shook her head furtively. "Must we talk about this now? You being here is putting a dampener on the whole evening."

Although subtle, Jay stiffened next to me, Helena Brandon's words rubbing him the wrong way as much as they did me. I felt the words rise up on to my tongue before I had a chance to stop myself.

"We hate to ruin your evening," I said, voice dripping with sarcasm and rising loud enough to catch the attention of the closest people to us, "but a member of your church congregation is dead, and from the information we have gathered, you and your husband appear to be some of the last people to see her alive. Maybe you would feel more comfortable if we went to the police station for a formal interview instead?"

"No," said Helena Brandon quickly, backtracking to the extreme. "I just meant–"

"We know what you meant, Mrs Brandon," Jay said. I gave Jay a look as he reached inside his pocket and pulled out a card with our office contact numbers on it. He offered it out. "We would appreciate finishing this conversation in the morning, either at the station or we can come to you. Give us a call."

Helena Brandon snatched it. "The only person you'll be talking to is my solicitor."

"If they can help us clear up the mystery surrounding Yvonne's death, then the more the merrier," said Jay.

Our exchange had caused quite a stir within the hall, and most of the audience were now looking our way, instead of taking their seats for the rest of the concert. Feeling a hundred pairs of eyes on me, I moved to the back of the hall with Jay, and when things finally settled down and the music restarted, we slipped out the back.

"That was uncomfortable," he remarked as we headed across the dark car park to our vehicles. The crispy leaves of the oak tree rustled overhead in the breeze. "You're not usually so snippy with people."

I prickled at his words. "And you're not normally so easy-going. She was hiding something. I refuse to believe Yvonne was a well-loved member of the church and they're all just carrying on as normal only a few hours after finding out she's dead. If we pushed her harder, we would have got somewhere."

"Maybe, or we would have been thrown out and then none of the congregation would talk to us."

"But they didn't tell us anything we don't already know. Yvonne started going there a year ago when her husband left her. It was a waste of time."

"It wasn't."

I placed my car key in the door lock and it clicked as it opened. Jay watched me for a moment, his gaze narrowing as he surveyed my movements.

"Are you still mad about the call-out this morning?"

I flicked my gaze skywards, wondering if the cloudy night could feel my frustration. Those little irritations I had assigned to the back of my mind were threatening to come back out again and merge into one big ball of anger. But ultimately, I knew why I was annoyed. It was because someone had viciously murdered a woman and these people were still carrying on as normal, drinking their ale and singing *Hungry like the Wolf.*

"No," I replied, releasing my anger into the night air. "This day just went downhill quickly. Tomorrow will be better."

Jay gave me a thin smile. "That's the spirit. Welcome to Serious Crimes, Anna. Where no case is straightforward."

"Night, Jay."

"Night, Anna."

## Chapter Four

I was still rubbing the tiredness from my eyes when I arrived at work the next morning, humming a Duran Duran song to myself and earning a glare from both of my colleagues for the earworm.

"Well," Chris said as he put down the phone and the printer spat out several pieces of paper. He still had his jacket on, however, so he hadn't been there long. "The entire world seems to be on a go-slow today. No preliminary pathologist report yet, no lab reports. We know no more than we did yesterday."

"Guess we'll just have to rely on our amazing detective skills," said Jay, keeping his gaze on his computer screen. "We're confident about the method, she was sliced across the throat. Has the murder weapon been confirmed?"

"Not yet, but there was a kitchen knife in the sink full of bleach, so that answer is fairly obvious. We need to get onto the lab today to chase those results."

Straight to it then, and with a brutal murder case on our hands, I guessed neither of them would want me to bring up the stupid hazing call-out they'd sent me to the day before. I sorted through the case file, looking for the images taken of the crime scene so they could be added to the sparse whiteboard.

"The knife block is missing a knife," I pointed out.

Chris nodded. "Yeah, I saw that too. If the killer took a knife from the knife block and used that to kill Yvonne, it suggests that they didn't plan to kill her, that it was a spur-of-the-moment crime."

"That's still a pretty brutal spur-of-the-moment crime," I said. "To cut someone's throat like that takes a lot of anger. What had Yvonne done to cause someone to attack her like that?"

"Who says she did something? She could have been the victim of a burglary gone wrong," said Jay.

"We can't rule anything out, but it's unlikely," said Chris. "There was no forced entry, and I didn't see anything worth stealing in that house. No, Anna is right, whoever did this was angry at our victim, enough to kill. We need to find out more about Yvonne to know who could possibly do this. Who could commit such a brutal act, and then manage to cover their tracks so well afterwards?"

"Well, the members of the church council should be coming by soon." Jay stretched and pushed himself away from his desk. "Mr and Mrs Brandon will hopefully be a bit more forthcoming today."

"Or their solicitors will just say 'no comment' to every question we ask," I mumbled under my breath. I wasn't holding out much hope that John and Helena Brandon were going to be any more cooperative. I could still picture Helena Brandon's expression of derision and her contempt at us daring to speak to her.

"That's good," Chris said. He hadn't heard me. "Let me know when they're here and I'll interview."

"No way, the Brandons are mine!" Jay protested. "I deserve a fair crack at them after that boring concert last night."

"Fine, we'll do it together."

"I wanted to interview!" I shot back.

"You can speak to the reverend," said Chris, carefully avoiding my gaze. "Nice, pious old man, should be fairly upfront. The Brandons sound like a trickier nut to crack."

"I can handle people like the Brandons." I bit my lip to stop myself from saying more. It seemed like the hazing and testing to join the Serious Crimes team wasn't over yet. Chris was the hardest to convince.

I grumbled under my breath, muttering a few swear words as Jay and Chris gathered up their case files and notebooks and headed downstairs to the interview rooms. Ten minutes later, I was called downstairs, where I found Reverend Harding waiting at the front desk. Today he wasn't dressed in his faded robes but in a loose woolly jumper with his dog collar sticking over the top.

"Detective McArthur." He greeted me with a warm smile and I showed him to a free interview room.

The starkness and sterility of the police station unnerved the reverend and he tugged at his collar as he sat down, eyeing up the posters on the wall. His gaze fell on the recording equipment as I flicked open my notebook.

"Don't worry, Reverend, this isn't a formal interview. We won't be needing that. We were hoping you could tell us some more about Yvonne, to help us find out who would do this to her."

A small smile of relief relaxed his face. "Oh good. I have to admit, I don't think I've been in a police station before. Not even when the lead was stolen from the roof of my last parish church. Ask away. I will help however I can."

"Great. When was the last time you saw Yvonne?"

"Saturday night," said the reverend confidently, grinning like he'd got the first question on the test correct. "We were all at the centre late rehearsing for the show. We finished up at about eleven, but Yvonne stayed a few minutes longer to tidy up. That wasn't unusual, she often did that and then locked up the building. I didn't see her on Sunday at the morning service, which I admit didn't really register with me until later."

"Who else was at the choir rehearsal?"

"Well, all the choir, including Yvonne; myself, not because I like to sing but I like to show my support; Helena and John Brandon, Helena directed the show; and young Jacob, their son, he moved all the chairs. I think that was all."

"What can you tell me about Yvonne? How long had she been coming to your church?"

"About a year," said Harding. "She took a job as cleaner of the community centre and church and started coming to events and services soon after. But it felt like she had always been there. She fit right in."

"What events specifically?" I asked.

The reverend tapped his fingers on his chin. "Well, every Sunday service, of course. She was a part of the choir, she helped with the pre-school groups and the coffee mornings. She even talked about wanting to set up her own group."

"Did she get along with everyone?"

Harding nodded enthusiastically. "Everyone. Everyone loved her. She was gradually coming out of her shell, after her divorce. She was working hard on finding happiness and that was admirable."

"What do you know about her divorce? Was her ex-husband still on the scene?"

Reverend Harding pursed his lips. "I've never met him. According to others in the flock, they'd lived just down the road for years but they were a reclusive couple, rarely sociable with their neighbours. Once her husband moved out, Yvonne put herself out there. She found a home with us at St Mary's."

"If she was such an integral member of the church community, why not cancel the choir concert last night?"

"Ah." Harding dropped his gaze, keen not to look me in the eye. "That was Helena's idea. She said Yvonne wouldn't want us to waste all our hard work. They've put hours into rehearsing for this concert. She said it would be a good way to honour Yvonne's memory."

I couldn't help but wrinkle my nose with disgust at this, making sure to blank my expression again in time before Harding looked up. "That's a bold way of honouring someone so soon after their death. Were Helena Brandon and Yvonne close?"

Harding shook his head slowly. "Not that I believed, but who knows. Maybe I wasn't privy to their private relationship. I have to have faith that everyone in my flock acts in the best interests of everyone else. I believe Helena does that."

Hmm, that was an odd way of looking at it, but I liked his positive outlook. It was unfortunate that such a positivity didn't usually apply to the crimes I investigated every working day.

"So, there isn't anyone in your flock who you believe could cause harm to Yvonne? No one who would want her dead?"

"No, of course not!" Reverend Harding pulled at his collar again, swallowing hard. "We are good, charitable people. I can say with good faith no one would have wanted to hurt Yvonne. You're looking in the wrong place."

\* \* \*

Chris and Jay were already back in the office when I returned, looking like boys who'd kicked their football over the fence.

"How did it go?" I contemplated not even asking the question, given that it was clear from their faces how well it had gone.

"No comment," replied Jay.

"That bad?"

"No comment. That was the most useful thing they said. No comment."

"Even to the easy questions?"

Chris grumbled under his breath, catching our attention. "Clearly, they are a family who have had bad experiences with police before. They toed the line between cooperative and uncooperative. But they did confirm what we've already been told about Yvonne. Recently divorced, relatively new to the church group. Everyone loved her, no one would want to hurt her. And if that was really the case, then we wouldn't be here now."

"So, you don't believe them?"

"Someone wanted to hurt Yvonne," said Jay as he leaned back in his chair. "The most obvious person is her ex. We should track him down."

"Agreed," said Chris and his gaze fell on me. "Anna?"

It wasn't an invitation to give my opinion, it was an indication to get going.

"I'll get started," I said with a sigh, and fired up my computer. The latest information on Keith Garrington was that he had run off to Spain, so I guessed that was the first place to look.

"Ooh." Jay rubbed his hands together. "What are the chances we have to jet off to sunny España to interview him? I could use a holiday."

"We've got to find him first. In the meantime, Jay, get onto the lab. We need those forensics reports back for the crime scene. We must consider canvassing the neighbourhood again, although yesterday's inquiries didn't bring back much. And get over to the morgue. We should at least have a preliminary pathologist report by now." Chris growled under his breath. "It's been twenty-four hours. We need something to show some progress, especially with Price breathing down our necks with his ridiculous deadline."

Chris's frustration was felt throughout the room, an unwanted reminder of the pressure on the Serious Crimes team. Three months before, the chief constable of the local police force had thrown his weight around and demanded a year-old murder case be solved within the next six months. Ali Burgess was a beautiful young woman who had met a violent end, and her killer had disappeared into the void. Despite our best efforts, the case was still wide open.

"We could ask for some more resources?" Jay offered.

Chris snorted back. "What resources? We're as short-staffed as the lab. Welcome to years of public funding being slashed," he said, giving a dismissive wave of his hands. "It's just the three of us for now. No pressure."

"No pressure at all…" Jay rolled his eyes.

Rather than get drawn into the pity party, I put my head down and ran every search I could think of for Keith Garrington. The results were mixed, leading me to believe that the story about him running away to Spain was true but the escape abroad was short-lived. In the last month, his name reappeared in the UK, linked to an address in North Norfolk, in the town of Aylsham. New car insurance policy, new utility bills. Everything pointed to him being back.

Just after midday, Jay slapped his hands on the desk and pushed himself away. "Right, my stomach is settled, time to visit the morgue."

"I have a possible address for Keith Garrington," I said. "Want to combine the visits?"

"Efficient," said Jay with a nod. He looked to Chris for approval, earning an apathetic shrug, which meant yes.

Jay drove us to the town's morgue, located in the depths of the local hospital, where we found Pete Kerry – the pathologist's assistant – singing away to the classic soft rock streaming from the radio in the corner of the room. There were three metal tables out in the unnaturally cool room, each one with a white sheet covering a familiar, unmoving shape underneath.

"Afternoon, Pete," said Jay, greeting the man and taking care not to look at the bodies on the tables too hard.

"Urgh, I was afraid you'd show up," replied Pete, but he quickly changed his tune with a scowl from Jay. "Not like that, sorry. I just mean, it's been a horrendous day. We've not even got around to your victim yet."

"What?" Jay's mouth fell open. "You're kidding me?"

"There was a three-car fatal accident in Watton yesterday, and an unexpected death on the post-op ward yesterday evening. The coroner hasn't even arrived yet. Oh, and the deputy pathologist is off sick."

"No…" Jay scuffed his feet, his disappointment radiating across the room. "Dear God, these staff shortages are killing us. Please tell me you've at least looked over the body. You must have something to tell us."

"Well, since it's you." Pete shuffled over to a stacked desk, prying a manilla folder from the pile and flipping it open. "I've had a little look over this morning. I'd say she passed away sometime Saturday night or early Sunday morning. Cause of death is most likely loss of blood due to the severing of the carotid artery. Slit throat, basically, with a sharp knife. There are signs of a mild struggle, a few bruises and such. Also signs that she lost a significant amount of weight recently. Lots of skin flaps."

"Matches with what the neighbours told us about taking in her dresses," I replied.

"I've sent samples from under her nails to the lab but don't hold your breath," Pete continued, "they're massively behind."

"So we've heard." With such a small amount to go on, Jay's expression crumpled into a malcontent scowl, and I saw a brief glimpse of the pressure that hung over the team to get a good result. He didn't need reminders of how difficult the task ahead was. "Well, if you find out anything else, let us know."

Pete returned to the nearest dead body, prepping some implements. From his tense exhale and refusal to meet Jay's gaze, he obviously wasn't expecting any more breakthroughs to help our case. "You'll be the first to know."

## Chapter Five

The town of Aylsham was a typical Norfolk town. Church, supermarket, almost identical bungalows and semi-detached houses with mature trees and tidy gardens. If I had been dropped in the middle of it by aliens, I wasn't sure I would be able to distinguish it from any other market town in the Norfolk and Lincolnshire area. However, it was a lively place whilst still holding onto its small-town charms, making it the perfect commuter base for Norwich.

Jay knocked heavily on the door of the run-down property on Yaxley's Lane, his thumps enough to garner the attention of the little old lady mogging down the street with her checkered trolley. However, there was no car in the driveway and no sounds from inside, so I didn't hold out much hope of this visit panning out. Nothing was going the easy way for us so far today.

After a few minutes of knocking, Jay gave up. "No one's home. Do you want to check round the back? I'll speak to the neighbours."

The semi-detached property had an alleyway leading down the side, overgrown with leylandii trees, and I fought my way through their prickly tendrils to the back garden. The garden gate lay on the ground, the hinges too rusty to hold it up. By the back door, the bins overflowed with beer cans and microwave meal trays. I peered in the windows but only found a sparse kitchen, with minimal cutlery and even more beer cans. No signs of life, just of a desperate existence.

At the bottom of the garden stood a shed, almost swallowed whole by the hedge. It was unlocked, but empty. The property shared a gate with its adjoining neighbour, although that too was almost overtaken by the hedge. Just as I closed the shed door, the gate creaked open a fraction.

"Oi! What d'you think you're doing?"

I spied a suspicious eye watching me through the gap, five feet from the ground. About two feet up, a brown muzzle sniffed the gap.

"I'm looking for Keith Garrington," I replied, holding my hands up to show them I wasn't a burglar. Not that this house looked like it had anything to steal. "Does he live here?"

"Aye," returned the cautious voice, northern accent thick and judging. "He's not here though. What do you want?"

The dog, a Rottweiler by its colouring, grizzled with its teeth clamped shut.

"Where can I find him?"

"Work. Not telling you where, though. You could be anyone."

"Well, I'm not anyone." I reached in my back pocket for my warrant card, but the action spooked the suspicious person and they flung open the gate.

I was met by a sturdy lady with permed hair. One hand was holding onto the collar of the dog, although from the way the dog tugged against her, it didn't look like she was having much luck holding it back.

"Stop!" she ordered me. "Put your hands where I can see them, or I'll let the dog go!"

"Relax, it's okay." I quickly put my hands in the air again. "It's okay, I'm police. I'm just getting out my ID to show you."

"Police?" She surveyed me a moment and then snorted. "No uniform. Surely, you're too overdressed to be police."

I wasn't sure what she meant, given that I was rarely overdressed. Today, I wore my standard black trousers, scuffed leather boots and thick jumper, the same orange colour as Jay's car.

"Well, we do have a dress code," I replied. "Just let me get out my ID and I'll show you."

I lowered my hand, but the dog didn't like that.

"Bruce, down!" the woman snapped, pulling hard on the dog collar. Bruce continued to pull, giving a low disgruntled growl as he eyed me hungrily.

"Miss, you really need to get that dog under control," I said trying to bite down on a slight panic that ignited at the snarl from the dog. I was a cat person for a reason. The jaws on that dog had the power to rip a limb off and I didn't fancy being the one it sunk its teeth into.

"It is under control, you're the one who's trespassing!"

"I'm not even in your garden!"

Bruce barked and the noise sent the birds flying from the trees. One short, sharp bark was enough to shut me up.

"I've had enough of this," declared the woman. "Get on the ground or Bruce will make you."

I tensed myself. I wasn't sure whether my best option was to run or get on the ground; although laying on the muddy, leaf-strewn garden wasn't appealing, it was better than being attacked by the dog. I'd watched enough police dogs in action to know that even the biggest, most cumbersome ones could run faster than a human. More often than not, dogs like Bruce weren't trained well and would readily snap a hand off whoever their owner told them to. People treated them more like a status symbol than a pet. Or worse, a weapon.

"One," warned the lady. "Two…"

"For fuck's sake, I'm going." I sunk down to my knees and prayed Jay wasn't close enough to see me at that moment. I'd never live it down.

"Three!"

I wasn't fast enough for the stern northern guard, and she released her grip on Bruce. Several stone of thick, muscled canine pounced forward on his short legs, letting out another bark. His mass propelled him forwards and he ran at me, no will to stop, and mouth hanging wide open, displaying rows of yellow-white fangs. Bruce collided with me and sent us both hurling to the ground.

I put my arms over my head, desperate to protect whatever part of me the teeth found first. But I was greeted by something wet and warm. It caressed my hands, then an equally wet nose nuzzled into my arms and found my face.

"Ah, Bruce," said the woman, sounding disappointed. "You great lump. Worst guard dog in the world."

Bruce released me momentarily, allowing me to sit up before he resumed his licking, and plastered a slobbery wet kiss right on my cheek. I scratched him behind his ears, which sent his tail wagging and, with the mighty beast defeated, I pulled my warrant card from my back pocket and showed it to the woman. With her fierce dog conquered so easily, her suspicion eased away and she helped me to my feet.

"Sorry, pet. I'm trying to train him to be more menacing. It's not working."

Bruce jumped on his hind legs and nuzzled his head into my arm, demanding some more attention. I gave the good boy another pet.

"Well, he's got the growling down at least," I said. "Although I can't say I approve of the use of a weapon for intimidation. Can you or Bruce tell me where I can find Keith Garrington?"

Not pleased with her pooch's poor performance, the woman crossed her arms and sighed. "I don't know. He hasn't lived here long, so I don't know him that well. He usually works nights at the airport, but he hasn't been home since Saturday."

"Since Saturday? What time on Saturday?"

She shrugged back, wrinkling her nose at Bruce. The dog's tongue lolled from the side of his mouth, and he rubbed against my leg, his tail whacking the back of my thighs as fast as a helicopter propeller. He gazed up at me with big brown eyes containing a type of adoration Poppy the cat never showed me.

"Dunno. Heard him go out early morning. Haven't seen him since."

"Can you tell me anything else about him? Anyone else live here with him, a girlfriend or partner?"

"No, he's on his own."

"Got his phone number?"

"No… but I can tell him you're looking for him."

Bruce the dog remained my biggest fan as I gathered some more details, including the name and contact details of the neighbour, and gave the woman a contact card to pass on to Keith. By the end of the conversation, he was sat at my heels, gazing at me with his adoring eyes. I bid goodbye to the neighbour who returned to her own garden and, to my surprise, Bruce followed me back to the front of the property.

"Bruce!" called his owner, "Bruce, come here! You daft dog, you live here!"

Jay was making his way back to his car from over the road and gave a bemused smile at my new companion. I stopped, and Bruce sat down again, his ears flopping with the movement. I gave him one last nuzzle under the chin.

"Go on, Bruce," I said gently and pointed back to the garden. "Go home."

And with his tail still wagging, Bruce trotted off back home. I climbed into Jay's car as he settled into the driver's seat.

"You made a friend?" he asked, still amused as he took in the mud now over my jumper and the leaf stuck in my hair.

"Could've been worse," I said, following his gaze and picking the leaf out. "My cat is more dangerous than Bruce."

\* \* \*

Evening was drawing over the station when Jay and I arrived back, making the sky look like a hastily coloured-in piece of paper, full of pink and orange. A keen breeze had whipped up, blowing the remaining leaves from the trees in persistent gusts. In an attempt to soften Chris's usual bad mood, we had stopped for decent coffee on the way and bought him one hoping it would make up for the lack of progress we had to show for the day. However, when we made our way to the Serious Crime office, we found Aaron also there, sitting across the room.

"That's my desk," I pointed out as Jay collapsed into his own with a hefty sigh. I left the warm cup on coffee in front of Chris, but he ignored it.

Aaron looked at Jay and me expectantly. "You can have it back if you've got some good news about the case."

"We haven't got much," replied Jay with a regretful frown. "Keith Garrington has been AWOL since Saturday, the day Yvonne was murdered. Not seen at home, his bosses report he hasn't been showing up for work. He's in the wind."

"Well, that's news, I suppose." Aaron's gaze fell on Chris. "Suspect number one. Chris has managed to pull together the documents from their divorce and they don't paint a pretty picture. He left behind a messy financial situation for his ex-wife."

Chris nodded and handed some paperwork to Jay. "She was in debt up to her eyeballs."

I peered over Jay's shoulder and gave a low whistle when I saw the red numbers on the bank statement he scanned over. And I thought my bank account was bad. Yvonne Garrington was steadily battling against the outstanding amount with her part-time job at the church but in the last year, it had barely made a dent.

"Right, next steps?" Aaron sat up in my chair. "Because it's two days into the investigation and there's not a lot to show for it. No forensic reports, no post-mortem. Just a handful of unhelpful witness accounts and a missing ex-husband."

"Chase the lab reports and put out an alert for Keith Garrington," said Jay, obviously.

Chris nodded along, the movement stiff. "We need to canvas the local area, get some media appeals going. Although we're facing the same issues as everyone else, there's not enough of us. We could use some extra bodies."

Aaron mulled this over for a moment. "You can have Maddie. That's all I can do; we're stretched thin already. However, this is a brutal and disturbing case in a seemingly close-knit community. We need to be seen as proactive."

"We are being proactive," I pointed out, and to prove my point, I waved at my muddy attire.

Aaron took a moment to look me over, before quickly avoiding my gaze and looking at Jay. "Do I even want to know?"

"She got attacked by a dopey dog. No harm done," he replied.

"I suppose Anna has to live up to the Crazy McArthur name somehow." Aaron pushed himself away from my desk and stood up, smoothing down his jacket. "But I'm serious, guys. We can't continue with nothing to show for this case. We need to find Keith Garrington. The longer a killer capable of doing this is free to walk the streets, the quicker the pressure will rise. He needs finding before Chief Constable Price has another excuse to scrutinise us."

"We're doing the best we can," I said.

Aaron's words made Chris and Jay bristle but they didn't argue back, apparently accepting that he was right.

"Well, it's not good enough," came the curt reply.

Earning moody grumbles of agreement back, Aaron exited the office, subtly brushing my arm as he passed. With a new heaviness over the room, I sank down into my seat, glancing at Chris and Jay, who looked equally as depressed as I felt. I fired up my computer, preparing myself to put in at least another two hours, when I spotted a folded sticky note on my desk. Hidden behind my glowing computer screen, I unfolded it.

*Free tonight?*

\* \* \*

I arrived home to my flat that evening to find Aaron waiting outside in his car, talking on his phone. The nights were pulling in fast, the drift of the dark purple sky overhead promising a chilly evening. The town was already half-asleep and the last of the commuter traffic pootled by, each driver looking as defeated by the day as I felt. Once finished, Aaron greeted me with a rare smile. I didn't return it.

"So," I said, turning my back on him to open the door to the building, "my best isn't good enough, huh?"

He groaned, throwing his head back as he followed me in. "I knew you'd be pissed about that. One day, when you're a DCI and have a team to lead, you'll understand how frustrating it is when your superiors are pushing for a result and your team have nothing to show."

"We don't have nothing," I replied as I began stomping up the two flights of stairs to my flat. Aaron trudged along behind. "We have a very good prime suspect."

"Who's gone AWOL," finished Aaron.

After letting us both in, I headed for the shower whilst Aaron got started on our evening meal, which was the least he could do, in my opinion. I emerged to find a delicious smell filling the flat, Poppy the cat happily chowing down on her food and Aaron idly flicking through his phone as he stirred the pan on the hob, which contained some sort of creamy mushroom sauce.

"Should we talk about the obvious?" I asked as I towelled my wet hair dry.

Aaron looked up briefly to give me a frown.

"What obvious?"

"The key thing," I said.

"Oh." He set aside his phone and turned down the dial on the hob to the lowest setting. "Well, there isn't really anything to say, is there? We manage just fine."

"Oh. I suppose so."

Aaron sighed heavily and stood up straight, loosened his tie until it was free from his neck. "You're angry with me now."

"No, I'm not… I was angry with you before."

"We're fine the way we are," he said, not quite able to hold my gaze. "We see each other a few times a week, a night at yours, a night at mine. It works. Any more and we risk the whole bloody station finding out. It's a miracle Maddie has kept her mouth shut this long."

He waited for my response, disappointed when I only gave a grumbling shrug back. I wasn't going to win this argument.

"What can I say to make it better?" he asked.

"Well, start by being nicer to me and I'll think about forgiving you."

"You know, I think you're amazing," he said, taking a step closer.

In my tiny flat, the kitchen was barely big enough for two people and I found myself pressed up against the fridge door. Aaron closed the gap between us, his body meeting mine.

I shook my head. "You don't tell me nearly enough."

"Really?" He pouted. "Okay, let me change that."

He passed his tie around the back of my neck and used it to pull me even closer before kissing me deeply. Every grumble I had slowly melted away as I let him press me into the cold fridge door, his breath becoming raspy within seconds. He let go of the tie and his hands wandered down until they found the edge of my dressing gown and ran underneath onto the warm skin of my thighs, still damp from the shower. He broke off the kiss when he realised that I had nothing else on.

"You *are* amazing," he breathed.

"I know," I replied. I let him slowly trace his hands over my skin as I undid the buttons on his shirt, one by one. Whatever was cooking was probably going to have to wait now, but as I pulled him closer for another kiss, I smiled to myself. I'd prove to him that I was good enough.

## Chapter Six

"Where's Chris?" PC Maddie Greene asked, stomping the mud from her boots onto the pavement. She'd met Jay and me at the end of Nelson Avenue the next morning, where some annoyingly dark clouds were starting to fill the sky and a blustering breeze still battered the trees. Apart from the obvious house surrounded in police tape waving in the wind, the rest of the street was subdued. The wind carried the sounds of construction work from the next street over, where two houses were being built. I could just spy the builders over the tops of the houses, standing on the scaffolding.

"The baby was ill in the night; she had a temperature," replied Jay, doing his best to hide his irritation. "He said he'd catch up with us after we've knocked on some doors."

I smiled to myself. Chris wasn't one to talk about himself and if it wasn't for Jay telling me, I wouldn't have known he had a family at all. Now I knew he was married with two teenage sons and then a little over a year ago, Chris and his wife Alicia were surprised by the arrival of unexpected baby number three, a pretty girl called Felicity. Chris gave me hope. If he could maintain a marriage and raise a family whilst doing this job – with its unsocial hours, grim cases and massive workload – then it was possible for any of us.

"All right for some," Maddie grumbled, which was actually a very good impression of Chris. "So, what's the plan?"

"We need to speak to the neighbours and see if anyone has spotted Keith Garrington in the area lately. Either before or after Yvonne's death," Jay said.

"Might be a good idea to check the other streets too," I said. "This area is full of cut-throughs, a lot of people use this street as a shortcut to the railway station."

"Good thinking," said Jay as he clicked his fingers. He was eager to get going. "Good use of local knowledge."

"Well, this is my home patch," I replied.

I stretched my arm, wincing at the twinge in my shoulder as I did. My old injury had been acting up all morning, somehow flared by being barrelled over by Bruce the dog the day before. Or maybe it was the late-night exercises with Aaron. Either way, I was regretting it today.

"You all right?" Maddie was watching me as I rolled my shoulder.

"Just my shoulder hurting. I'm not as fit as I used to be. I need to get back to exercising."

"You can join me for an early morning jog," she said, a devilish grin crossing her face. Nothing about the words 'early morning jog' sounded appealing though. "Anyway, I'll start over at the building site on Snape Lane, see if they've seen anything lately."

"As you're the local history guru, Maddie," I said, "do you know why this town has so many things named after Nelson?"

She wrinkled her nose at me. "Huh?"

"Nelson Avenue; the primary school is called Nelson School. The Trafalgar Industrial Estate."

"Well," said Maddie. "It's after Admiral Lord Nelson, isn't it?"

Jay gave a bewildered look between the two of us, confused by the change of topic. "Yeah, everyone knows that. Norfolk. Nelson's county."

"Yes, I know that," I replied. "But why?"

"Nelson was born here. He went to school in the town," said Maddie.

"Did he?"

"Well, apparently."

"Done discussing history?" asked Jay, waving his hand with impatience. "Let's get going then."

We set off, armed with photos of Keith Garrington and his car, and for the next two hours Jay and I scoured Nelson Avenue in search of a neighbour that could confidently say they had seen him in the area around the time of Yvonne's death. But because life was never easy like that, our inquiries turned up nothing.

Jay and I regrouped at the end of the street and looked at the community centre of St Mary's Church. Both the church and the community centre were locked up, although my local knowledge told me there would be a yoga class there that afternoon. We would just have to come back if we wanted to catch the church community, and pray in the meantime that they might be more helpful this time around.

With the oak leaves falling in the rustling breeze, I remembered my days in uniform, making regular stops in the area to catch the local teens out. It became kind of a dance at times; they'd see me coming and scarper, I'd pop by when they least expected it. I lost more times than I won, but when I caught them, it was worth it.

"When I worked on the Neighbourhoods team," I said to Jay, "we always had a problem with teens hanging out in the community centre car park. Around the back, it's overgrown and the perfect hideout. They'd be doing the usual, drinking, smoking, but occasionally there'd be complaints of noise or vandalism. What if someone was hanging out when Yvonne was killed and saw or heard something?"

He chewed over the suggestion. "It's the middle of the day, shouldn't they be in school?"

"Of course they should, but don't tell me you never bunked off school." I flashed Jay a grin, which he didn't return. "I used to skip out at lunchtime, stop off at the shop for sweets and meander my way through the park as slow as I could with my boyfriend of the time."

"Ooh, you rebel." Jay tutted but waved his hands for me to lead the way.

At the entrance to the car park, I paused, listening for any sounds of life. I heard a scuffle and crisp crunch of leaves as a young boy of around twelve appeared, hurrying from the overgrowth at the back of the community centre. He ran, looking desperately behind him like there was a monster on his tail, and crashed straight into Jay.

"Woah!" he said, as the young lad went flying to the floor. His oversized school bag weighed him down and Jay picked the boy back up, setting him on his feet. "What's the hurry?"

"Nothing," the boy squeaked, still looking behind him with worried glances. "Sorry."

He pushed past Jay, pumping his feet fast, but ducked his head a little too late to disguise the tears in his eyes.

"I think they're home," I said to Jay with a grin.

"Who?"

"You'll see."

Charging on ahead so that he had no choice but to follow, I led Jay around the back of the community centre and through a path forged through the undergrowth of shrubs and brambles behind the building. Emerging on the den, I found it occupied by three older teenage boys. Two were sat on a grungy old leather sofa. The other leaned on a pile of pallets, possibly meant to be a makeshift table. They all stiffened at our arrival, regarding us warily.

"What do you want?" said the closer lad, who was standing against the pallets.

He took a few steps forwards, squaring up to me as if I would find his shaved head and skinny face intimidating. I definitely did not.

After a second, his eyes flashed with recognition.

"PC Mac!" he said, his face filling with a cheeky sheen. "I haven't seen you in ages. I thought you retired."

"No such luck," I said with a grimace.

Brady Boston was well known enough in the area as a general delinquent. A young lad from a less-than-desirable home, he spent most of his time causing trouble one way or another. I couldn't believe that after several years, he could still be found hanging around this dingy den, smoking and drinking with his friends. As a youngster he thought himself the big bad boss of the gang. Clearly that hadn't changed.

"What are you up to, Bos?" I asked, remembering that he'd be more likely to smack me if I called him Brady.

As Bos regarded Jay with a suspicious glare, I sidled around him and inspected the two on the sofa. Both held cans of lager. One of them I didn't know, but the other, who shrunk down into his hoodie under my gaze, seized my attention.

"Jacob?" I asked, wondering what on earth Jacob Brandon was doing hanging out with someone like Bos. From our first meeting at the church group's choir concert, I had thought him to be a helpful, sincere lad. If the company he kept was anything to go by, I was wrong.

"You know her?" the other lad asked, nudging Jacob.

"No!" the teen replied quickly, but even under his hood I could see his face flush a rosy, red colour.

"Come on, officer, leave my mates alone," Bos said, appearing at my side. He threw his arm around my shoulder in an attempt to get me to move away and usher me to the entrance of the den. I threw his arm off. "We're not doing anything, swear it. We're just chilling."

I wasn't fooled by his boyish charm. "I'm still a copper," I said, and watched as Bos's face sank. "I might not be in uniform, but I'm still an officer. And you know how I feel about underage drinking in a public place."

Jay, catching my drift, took the cans of lager from the group and proceeded to pour the contents away.

"Aw, come on!" Bos protested.

"Sit." I gestured to the sofa and with a grumble under his breath, Bos sat down. So much for the big gang leader.

"I'm eighteen next week," he said. "You can't do jack shit then."

"Bos, I've been catching you drinking around here since you were twelve. You need to find a better hobby. Whose phone is that?" I motioned to the mobile phone he held in his hand. It was immaculate, with a back case depicting some sort of computer game I knew nothing about. I doubted it belonged to him.

"No one's."

"So, it's not yours?"

"I didn't say that."

"Then is it yours?"

"I found it," Bos said stiffly. "Someone must have dropped it."

I held out my hand for it. "Like that young lad you just scared off, the one who stumbled out of your hideout? Hand it over. I know how sticky your fingers can be."

Bos swore at me. "I forgot how annoying you were. You always assume I'm doing something wrong, whatever I'm doing."

"That's because I nearly always catch you in the middle of doing something wrong," I said. "And illegal. Now, sit still. I'm not here to chastise you for underage drinking or whatever. I want to ask you some questions."

Bos glanced at his friends before crossing his arms and giving me and Jay a look of disdain. He was definitely the ringleader of the group, as Jacob and the other lad copied his expression of disgust.

"Where were you Saturday night, when the concert rehearsals were going on in the community centre?"

Bos shrugged. "I was here with some friends. Ben was here too. Jacob's a pansy and wouldn't say no to his parents so he was in the hall, singing his heart out."

"I wasn't singing!" Jacob protested but Bos just sniggered at him.

"And what time did you leave?" Jay asked.

"Dunno. About two."

"Did you hear anything strange or out of sorts on that night?"

"No." Bos eyed Jay carefully, his gaze flitting over to me occasionally. He knew me, albeit only as an authoritative force constantly on his back, but he still knew me enough to remember the little nickname he'd given me. But he didn't know Jay at all.

"Bos, it's all right," I said. "This is Jay, we work together. We're investigating the death of the woman who lived down the road."

The skinny young man raised his eyebrows at me. "You mean the one who got her throat slashed?"

I nodded and wrinkled my nose. "Yeah. How did you know that?"

"Jacob told me," Bos said quickly.

"My parents told me!" Jacob said even faster. Then the gang fell quiet.

"Gruesome, isn't it," I said. "Anything you can tell us could be helpful. Did you hear anything unusual? Any arguments?"

Bos appeared to give his answer more thought this time. "No, we didn't."

"What time did everyone leave the community centre?"

"I dunno. Midnight? We didn't hear anything unusual, just their awful singing all bloody night."

Ben sniggered and Jacob elbowed Bos. Between the three of them, I couldn't see any obvious signs of lying, though I knew Bos could charm the pants off a nun if he really wanted to. But since they had nothing to hide apart from a few cans of cheap booze, I was inclined to think that Bos and his gang were telling the truth.

"All right," I said. "Last one. Have you seen this man before?"

I showed the trio a picture of Keith Garrington, but all three shook their heads.

"Well, if you think of anything else, you know where to find me."

Jay and I backed off, heading for the exit. Bos leapt straight to his feet, eager to see me off.

"Oh, I know where to find you," he said, practically pushing me away. "I'll just do something bad and you'll appear, like magic, like you always do."

"I'd rather you just called," I replied, and gave him a card with our office number.

Bos hastily shoved it in his pocket. "Yeah, yeah, fine. See you never, hopefully."

\* \* \*

Chris was in the office when we made it back at lunchtime, although by the dark bags under his eyes, what Jay had said about his sleepless night had been true. Recognising the need for caffeine, Maddie offered to make a round of drinks and Jay filled Chris in on our morning.

The sleep-deprived team leader grunted at our lack of progress. "No one can remember seeing Keith Garrington in the area? At all?"

Jay shook his head. "Not recently. Quite a few neighbours recognised him from when he lived there, but no one recalled him being back at the house in the last few months at least."

"Is this man some sort of master spy? How has he dropped off the grid so well? I've checked in with the local Aylsham bobbies, he hasn't been home since your visit yesterday. His car hasn't been picked up anywhere, no pings on his credit card… It's like the man has vanished into thin air."

"He's a hefty man," said Jay as he looked at a photograph of Keith Garrington we had stuck on the whiteboard of progress. "I can't see him vanishing anywhere. Where else can we try? We could ask the church group if they remember seeing Keith in the area lately?"

"Anna can do that; I want you to get onto the lab. We're still missing those reports."

Jay groaned. "You know they won't send them over for me. They need a call from a grumpy, overstressed senior officer. DI or higher."

"All right, I'll do it," Chris said. "You can inform Aaron of our lack of progress for the morning."

"Urgh. Fine, I'll do it," Jay said quickly, picking the lesser of the two evils.

Maddie returned with a tray of steaming hot beverages and a pack of biscuits, which denoted how poorly the case was going – the biscuits were only cracked out on bad days. I scanned through my emails as I took a sip of the burning hot coffee and let it scald its way down my throat. The pain felt reassuring, a stark reminder that no matter what death and deceit I faced in my job, I was alive and well. I'd let myself get bogged down in a case before, letting it affect my mind and mood, and I didn't want to go down that path again.

I had a dozen emails, nearly all of them wanted some sort of attention and action. One stood out though.

"Have you seen the email from the Comms team?" I asked Chris and Jay.

"Not yet," Jay replied. "What does it say?"

"It's only just come in. They received a call in relation to the case about twenty minutes ago. An anonymous tip-off that Keith Garrington was seen on Nelson Avenue on Saturday night, the night of Yvonne's murder."

Both Chris and Jay sat up, like meerkats on alert. They glanced at each other, mirroring confused frowns at this new information.

"Really? It names Keith Garrington?"

"It does," I said with a nod. "The caller refused to give their details and the number couldn't be traced." I took another deep sip and waved my hand at Maddie to hand me a biscuit. "That can't be right though. We've just spoken to that whole street, no one can remember seeing Keith Garrington in over a year. There's no doorbell cameras or CCTV nearby."

"If it's true, it's a good breakthrough," said Chris.

"But who could it have come from? If not the neighbours."

"The church group," Jay said. "They were all there Saturday night, rehearsing. Maybe one of them saw him as they were leaving."

"But we've already asked Reverend Harding and Mr and Mrs Brandon about Yvonne's husband. They said he was absent from her life."

Chris clicked his fingers, either signalling for a biscuit or to get our attention. "But we haven't asked all of them. Okay, change of plan. Anna, chase up the lab reports. Jay and I will call the church group members and try to track down where this anonymous lead has come from."

I opened my mouth to respond, to make clear how I didn't agree and how all this felt a bit too convenient, but Maddie anticipated me and shoved another biscuit in my hand. Her meaning was clear, and I closed my mouth. I was heading back down the route of being negative. I needed to let it go, trust my superiors, and ultimately do what they said. It was one of the first things Chris had said to me on joining this team; 'you do what we say, when we say'.

Swallowing my bruised pride, I crunched the biscuits and let the crumbs rain down on my keyboard. My computer pinged with a new email, the notification popping up on the screen, begging for my attention.

*Simon Hartley – Victim Support Team*
*URGENT – FAO DC McArthur – upcoming parole board hearing*

Aware of Maddie just a few feet away from me, I quickly closed the notification. The email still sat unread in my inbox, and it would stay there for now. There was only one reason the Victim Support team would contact me and I wasn't prepared to allocate it any headspace now or any time soon.

## Chapter Seven

"What sort of time is this?" I asked, sleep still tugging at my eyes. I was dressed, stretched and waiting outside, before the sun had even had a chance to shine over the rooftops of the building on the side street where I lived. My building was an old shop, separated into three flats now with parking for several cars in front. At this ungodly time of the morning, I could hear the distant bustle of the town as it woke up, but my quiet corner remained resting.

My companion reached me, yawning loudly as she walked. Maddie stretched her arms, rolling her eyes at me with a level of derision I always expected from her. "You're the one who wanted to come on a jog with me this morning. It's not my fault my shift starts at seven." She gazed around, standing on one foot to stretch her calf muscles. "Is that Aaron's car?"

She pointed to the silver SUV parked next to my rusty VW Golf, which somehow still had fallen oak leaves stuck on its roof from its trip to the community centre at St Mary's Church.

"Yeah. He's still asleep."

"Oh." Maddie looked at me with a mischievous grin. "I'm glad you patched things up. I thought you had reconciled – everyone has been pointing out what a good mood the boss has been in the last few weeks."

Although becoming a good friend and confidante, I reminded myself that Maddie was also the police station's biggest gossip and driving force behind the rumours that fuelled everyone's day. She had kept her mouth shut about Aaron and me so far, but I had nothing but her word that she would keep our secret.

"Come on then, let's get this over with."

"What's made you suddenly want to get fit?" she asked.

I shrugged, feeling a prickle of hot self-consciousness rise up my neck. "I used to be a lot faster on my feet back when I was in uniform with you. CID has dampened my reflexes."

I rolled my shoulder, the injured one that still occasionally twinged with pain when I least expected it. The truth was that I was mad at myself for how inactive I'd become. After being stabbed, and then the altercation with Greg Hanson leaving me with a broken arm, I would not let myself suffer any more ill fates due to my own lack of fitness.

"Come on, let's go. One lap around town."

We set off at a steady pace, Maddie keeping it slow just for me. I was so out of practice that it was embarrassing, but thankfully Maddie made no comment. We jogged through the quiet streets of Downham Market, through the town centre and back out again to the suburbs of old terraces and new-build estates. At this time in the morning, only the delivery truck for the newsagents on Bridge Street and commuters so tired they could have been zombies graced the streets.

As we jogged through the town, heading for the river on the west side, I paused at a junction to tie my shoelace. Maddie paused too, panting for breath as she watched me.

"You're not that out of shape," she remarked.

I stood up straight. My lungs were burning like I'd swallowed hot coals. "I feel like I am."

We had paused at the top of Nelson Avenue, looking down the street towards the church and community centre. There was lots of old cut-throughs and alleyways around this part of town, passageways to get from one road to another.

Maddie turned to me and clicked her fingers, something lighting up her eyes.

"Burnham."

I frowned back at her, pressing my hand into the stitch in my side. "Huh?"

"Horatio Nelson wasn't from Downham Market. He was from one of the Burnhams... Thorpe, I think. Anyway, I was close. Still Norfolk, but wrong town."

"Okay," I replied. "But that still doesn't explain why Downham has these roads named after him. Weren't there any other historical figures from the town to name things after?"

Maddie chewed this over for a minute, digging deep into her reserves of useless knowledge, before shaking her head in conclusion. "No. There's none."

"No one famous from this town at all?"

"Mmm, no. Not really."

"All right then."

As Maddie looked around, something caught her eye further along, near Yvonne Garrington's property.

"What's going on over there?"

She pointed to a small blue car parked on the roadside, outside Yvonne's house. Voices floated down the tarmac towards us, one gruff and defensive, the other firm and no-nonsense. Without much hesitation, I headed towards it, easily drawn to the only other people awake at this time in the morning. I heard Maddie tut behind me as she followed.

Robert Welles, Yvonne's nosy neighbour, was leaning over the garden wall between their two properties, telling off someone in Yvonne's front garden. An imposing man, with broad, body-builder shoulders and torso to match, fiddled with the front door to the property. He had dark shaggy hair and beard, and growled at Robert Welles as the latter chided him.

"It's an active crime scene," Robert Welles said, not spotting Maddie and me approaching. "No one is allowed in there."

"It's my bloody house!" the stranger argued back.

I cleared my throat, startling both the men. "Mr Garrington, I presume," I said and beside me, Maddie fished out her mobile phone. "We've been looking for you."

"What are the chances?" Maddie mumbled to herself, throwing me a look.

The man snapped upright and gave me a wary glare, flexing his hand around a battered old key. "Who are you?" he asked, eyeing me and my colleague in our workout clothes.

"Detective Constable Anna McArthur. I'm investigating your ex-wife's death. I'm afraid you're going to have to come down to the station to answer a few questions."

Over the garden wall, Robert Welles gave Keith Garrington an unsympathetic shrug. "I told you, you weren't allowed in there."

Keith Garrington surveyed the scene for a moment; Robert Welles' head and torso were poking above the parapet of the garden wall, and Maddie and I were standing on the pavement at the crime scene tape, like it was a finish line. We had him surrounded. If he fiddled with that door lock one more time, I'd be tempted to vault right over the tape.

His body tensed. He glanced around, like prey looking for an escape from a predator.

"Don't even think about it, Mr Garrington," I warned. Maddie was talking softly into the phone, signalling for backup.

He flexed his knees. He was going to run.

"Don't," I said one more time, but it fell on deaf ears.

With the spriteliness of someone half his age, Keith Garrington pushed his way from the front door and jumped over the crime-scene tape in one easy leap. He barged past Maddie, sending her toppling over, and was off down the street like a marathon runner. With a hefty sigh, I started after him.

"Anna!" I heard Maddie call after me, and the sound of footsteps pounding told me she'd picked herself back up and was following.

Keith Garrington's running stance didn't last long as soon his unfitness turned him into a lumbering animal rather than a sprinting champion. He clearly knew this area well, however, as he took a quick left and darted down an alleyway hidden beside another set of terraced cottages. Gravel skidded beneath my feet as I followed. My lungs burned in protest at more exercise but I pushed on, determined not to let a man in his fifties the size of a house outrun me.

I knew this area well too, and I knew that Keith was either trying to lose me in the town's old, terraced streets or heading for the newer housing estate, where all the roads were named after trees. A quick turn down Elizabeth Avenue. For many years I had patrolled round here, chased miscreant youths down these pavements, and I knew Keith Garrington ultimately had nowhere to go.

He seemed to come to the same conclusion as he slowed at the end of the street before taking another abrupt left. I heard Maddie puffing behind me, although the sound was soon lost to the pumping of my own blood through my ears. At the end of the road was one of the main throughfares of the town, the odd car rolling down the road as the residents started to awaken. Keith disappeared from our view as he rounded the corner of an old shop, onto the one-way street.

Just as I slowed to take the corner, the pavement far too narrow for anything other than an ant, I heard the chug of an engine. A van appeared in front of me, turning down the street with too much haste. Its tyres screeched as the startled driver slammed on the brakes.

"Watch out!" Maddie yelled behind me, and her hands found my arms and shoved me to the side. Both of us crashed into the carrstone wall of the old shop, the rock grating into my exposed skin. The van squealed to a stop, inches from our legs.

I glanced over Maddie, relieved to see that she was okay too, just with flakes of brickwork in her hair and a flushed red face. With a nod, we reassured each other and rounded the corner, ready to take on Keith Garrington once more.

Fortunately, we didn't have to go far.

Just round the corner, on the doorstep of the old shop, sat Keith with his head in his hands, breathing heavily.

"I give up, I give up!" he cried, throwing his hands in the air, but they didn't stay up for long before they collapsed back down.

Maddie waved her hand at me, also tenderly rubbing a spot in her sternum. "You do the honours."

I licked my desert-dry tongue around my lips. "Keith Garrington… you're under arrest for tampering with a… crime scene… Anything you do say…"

Keith Garrington flopped his hand at me. "Yeah, yeah, we get the point, love."

\* \* \*

Either he was secretly pleased with my collar or he was fed up with me asking, but Chris agreed to let me interview Keith Garrington. Whilst I was pumped with excitement, Jay grew frustrated and kicked the wall of the corridor as we waited outside the interview room. Keith Garrington's solicitor had insisted on speaking to him alone before we started.

"Are you sure there are no previous records for this guy?" Jay asked, already knowing what my answer would be.

"Yes," I said again. "I checked everywhere. Why, were you expecting something?"

"Well, yeah," he replied with a shrug. "The murder was brutal, nothing accidental about it. It's not often someone reaches that level of violence without there being warning signs before. And we already know Yvonne and Keith's marriage didn't end happily. He left her for another woman."

"Just because it wasn't a good break-up, doesn't mean domestic violence was involved," I said.

"But was there really not a single call-out? Even with neighbours like the Welleses just next door, there wasn't a single report of disturbances, arguments – nothing?" asked Jay.

"No," I confirmed, starting to doubt whether I had conducted the check correctly now. "There was nothing to suggest their marriage had been violent, Jay. I guess we'll just have to ask him."

"You ask," he said. "I'll chip in when we hit a nerve."

Jay's kicking was starting to leave a scuff on the wall, but it was only one of many blemishes where annoyed service users had taken their frustrations out on the innocent décor. I caught him glance at me.

"Have you done many investigations involving domestic violence, Anna?"

Within a split second, Jay's attention was on me, waiting for my answer. I must have given away my distaste of that sort of crime. I had a stomach of steel when it came to messy deaths, but domestic violence cases were a weak point. My hatred of those who abused their partner was just as strong as my hatred of solicitors, and also came from a similar place of personal experience.

"I've worked a few," I said carefully. "Nothing that resulted in a death."

"It's one of those crimes many victims are ashamed of," said Jay. "It's an angle we need to bear in mind. Whoever killed Yvonne Garrington was someone she knew well enough to let into her house, as there was no forced entry. And someone whose relationship with her was contentious enough to result in that level of violence."

I gave a hum to show him my agreement, but my mind wandered off to the place where I hid all those unwanted memories. Just before I became lost, reliving things I would rather forget, the door to the interview room opened and the duty solicitor motioned us in, the consultation over. As Jay and I settled into the cold chairs of the interview room, Keith sat opposite us. He regarded me with thinly concealed contempt, not pleased to see me again, and still flushed and mangled from his impromptu marathon. Even the duty solicitor sat next to him looked scared of the man, a solid force of middle-aged fat and muscle with a formidable stare.

After Jay started the recording and informed Keith Garrington of his rights, he sat back to let me ask the first questions.

"What were you doing at Yvonne's house, Mr Garrington?" I asked.

"Yvonne's house?" Little flecks of spit landed on the table between us as he spoke, anger appearing far quicker than I expected. "That's *my* bloody house. We bought it together."

"You left," I said, amazing myself with my calm tone. "You left Yvonne, along with a mortgage six months in arrears. We've reviewed Yvonne's finances; you left her in a precarious position. But you knew that, didn't you? You knew you left her with a lot of debt."

"My name's still on the deed, it's still my property. If I want access in there, you can't stop me."

Even the solicitor shook his head a little at this.

"Actually, I can," I said. "Your wife was brutally murdered inside it. Why did you want to go in?"

"I wanted to see if it was true," Keith replied as he balled his fists up.

"Really? You could have just asked. It's a good job I stopped you when I did, because you were about to walk right into the worst crime scene I've seen in my career."

Keith Garrington sat back in his seat. For a moment, his face dropped. "She's really dead?"

I nodded and out the corner of my eye, I could see Jay nodding too. We let Keith absorb the news for a minute, no sound interrupting the stillness of the room other than his shuddering breaths. I shuffled in my seat and drew his attention back to me.

"Mr Garrington, where were you between 10 p.m. on Saturday and 8 a.m. on Monday?"

He blinked at me, taking a moment to catch my meaning. "You mean, did I kill her? No… No, I didn't. Why would I kill Yvonne?"

"Where were you between those times?"

"Probably at home," he said. His shock at Yvonne's death passed and the irritated undertone in his voice reappeared. "I spent all day at home, in Aylsham. I haven't been to Downham in almost a year."

"That's not what your neighbour told us. They said you haven't been home since Saturday morning and your workplace said you haven't turned up for work since then either. Can anyone confirm where you were at any point during those times?"

Keith shook his head. "No. I was alone. But that doesn't mean I killed Yvonne!"

"How did you find out about Yvonne?" Jay asked, drawing Keith Garrington's ferocious glare to him.

"I don't know. I don't remember."

"Can you see where our suspicion is coming from?" Jay continued. "You can't account for your whereabouts at the time of the murder. You split from Yvonne, and from what we've heard so far, it wasn't a happy marriage. You left her with a lot of debt and ran off with another woman. These are all factors that would've caused a lot of contention between the two of you."

"I didn't kill her," Keith said again, more firmly this time. "If anything, *she* would've killed *me* if she had the chance."

"Did you two have a violent relationship?" I asked. "Were there often fights that got physical, or even threats to turn physical?"

Keith looked appalled at me. "No. Look, Yvonne and I didn't like each other, we certainly didn't love each other by the end. But we were never violent to each other. Never."

I made a note but didn't offer any further acknowledgment. I had seen far too many domestic cases where the perpetrator – and often even the victim – swore blind that they would never hurt another person. Maybe I was just getting sceptical. This job did have that effect on people.

Keith Garrington took my silence as a sign to carry on. "I know you'd love to pin this on me, the scumbag ex who dumped her, but the truth is that you don't know what Yvonne had been up to this last year, and neither do I. When we were together, she was a recluse, she never left the house. I've heard she's changed a lot since I left; got herself some new friends, lost a lot of weight."

From my impressions of Yvonne, what Keith said did appear to be true. From the outside, Yvonne appeared to be someone who had found a new lease of life since her divorce.

"What was your relationship like? Particularly towards the end," I asked.

Keith shrugged and sank down in his seat. "We got married when we were eighteen, right out of school. That was thirty-five years of everything being the same. The same meals every week, the same conversations, the same fights. God, it was hell, but I didn't even know it was hell until I met AJ. She was so fun and lively. She made me see the light."

"And how did Yvonne take it when you told her about AJ?"

"How do you think? She cried, screamed, threw my clothes in a suitcase and told me to get out."

"Well, that doesn't sound like a healthy relationship," remarked Jay.

I expected Keith's anger to rear its head again, but the opposite happened. The very last piece of fight left him, and I saw a broken man. A man who had turned his back on the past and was now realising just how final life could be.

"I've got no reason to kill Yvonne. I left her, I ended it and that was the last we spoke. We may not have liked each other but I wouldn't wish her harm. We were both just happy to finally be… rid of each other."

## Chapter Eight

Chris slammed his hand down on the desk, rattling his empty coffee mug and tipping over his pen pot. "What do we know about this guy?"

The clock was ticking. Since arresting Keith Garrington, we had only a finite amount of time to keep him in custody and grill him regarding Yvonne's death. As soon as he was released, we ran the risk of him disappearing again. We needed to piece the evidence together before the clock ran out and we had to let him go. Unfortunately, our evidence was still out for processing.

"Keith Garrington, age fifty-four," I read out from the case file. "No previous convictions. Currently works as a baggage handler at Norwich airport, mostly the night shift. Divorced Yvonne a year ago and ran off to Spain with a woman named Alyssa-June Masters."

"Have we tracked her down yet?" Chris asked, clicking his fingers at Jay. He was about two minutes away from pacing the room.

"We've tried, I think she's still abroad," replied Jay. "I've sent off a request to the Spaniards, but they're probably all still on siesta."

Chris grumbled under his breath. "We've only got him for eighteen more hours before we have to charge him. I want him charged with this murder rather than just tampering with a crime scene. Anna, how are you getting on with the lab?"

"We've got a few reports back," I replied, hoping that would be good enough. "The knife had no residual DNA on it, no fingerprints recovered. Same with Yvonne's mobile phone, both of which were found in the sink, covered in bleach. No data was recoverable. Still waiting on the rest of the forensics reports from the scene. If we get lucky, there might be DNA or fingerprints from something like the glasses or the mug found by the body."

That sent Chris to his feet and started off the pacing. The tick of the clock grew louder, as if the device knew our urgency and wanted to remind us of how pressed we were.

"That's not fucking helpful." Chris rubbed his chin as he paced. "Maddie, get over to the lab and bang down the door until they give us something we can pin on him."

"On it," she replied and she jumped to her feet, eager to get moving again.

I envied Maddie as she made her escape from the office.

"I've been taking a closer look at Yvonne's financial records," said Jay, shuffling some of the papers on his desk. In the last few hours, the papers had taken over every inch of space. "I've got some things I want to ask Keith about. So, he left Yvonne to cover the mortgage, which was already six months in arrears after Keith lost his job the year before. When he ran off, he took the last of his redundancy payout with him."

"Was Keith still named on the mortgage?" Chris asked.

"He was. And because of their insurance, Keith's now the owner of the house. The mortgage will be paid in full with Yvonne's death."

Chris rubbed his chin thoughtfully. "That's quite an incentive to wish her dead. What's Keith's current financial situation like?"

"Not great, but not as bad as Yvonne's," I replied, handing over Keith Garrington's bank statements to Jay. "The airport doesn't pay too badly."

Jay scanned them, comparing to Yvonne's documents he had in front of him. "Yvonne managed to negotiate with the bank to repay the outstanding mortgage arrears and she was making payments. However, her job at the church cleaning wouldn't have been enough to pay that and her other bills. It definitely doesn't look like Keith was contributing. She must have been getting an income from somewhere else."

"Like where?" Chris demanded.

"Not a clue. It must have been cash because it hasn't gone through her bank. All indications are that Keith was always the breadwinner whilst they were married, but Yvonne had a few part-time jobs over the years. Mostly admin. She was barely staying afloat without him."

"Okay," said Chris, "that's a point but it doesn't help us now. Keith Garrington isn't likely to know where Yvonne was getting her extra money from, he was too busy shagging his new girlfriend in Spain. Messy finances might not be enough to get him though, it's too coincidental. What else can we get him on right now?"

"Jealousy?" I offered. "Maybe Keith tried to get Yvonne back."

Jay shook his head. "By the accounts of everyone we've spoken to so far, Yvonne had moved on. She lost weight, made new friends, changed her style. And Keith left her in the shit. She wouldn't let him back in and there's no evidence they'd had any contact either."

"And we can't pin him at the scene yet," concluded Chris with another growl of frustration.

Jay sifted his papers, dropping his gaze to the floor. He cleared his throat and turned to Chris. "There is one more thing."

Chris paused his pacing. "Well? Spit it out."

"I ran a search on the address and found some old results. Three call-outs for domestic disturbances, all over ten years ago."

"Three?" Chris asked, before flicking his gaze over to me. "How did we miss that? I thought you'd ran a search on the address and Keith Garrington?"

"I did," I said earnestly. "I swear. It returned no results."

"I think I know what happened," said Jay. "It's 2 Churchside Cottages, not 2 Nelson Avenue. You ran the wrong address."

The ensuing silence was filled with the ticking of the obnoxious clock, almost mocking me with its relentlessness. Chris's already surly gaze turned on me, steadily growing wilder with ill-contained anger. Unable to escape it, I shrank down in my seat and Jay continued to explain.

"There were no convictions, so Keith Garrington doesn't have a criminal record, but the call-outs were all made by concerned neighbours, worried about violence occurring. Responders saw no evidence and neither Keith nor Yvonne cooperated, so the calls were closed."

"Fucking hell…" Chris rolled his eyes, throwing his arms in the air. "We missed *that*! A history of suspected domestic violence linked to our suspect and victim. Bloody hell, Anna, you should've found that earlier."

At least Jay had the good grace to not look at me as I felt my cheeks burn with embarrassment. Chris was right, I should've found that and I was more than annoyed at myself for missing it. I was better than that... well, I should've been.

"Sorry" was all I could say, and I wasn't even sure Chris heard it over his huffing.

"Right," he said, ignoring me and talking directly to Jay. "We've got a slight piece of leverage now, Garrington claimed there was no violence between him and Yvonne. We need to press him until he confesses otherwise. Previous domestic violence, he left her in a heap of debt. Imagine if he tried to worm his way back in only to find Yvonne had moved on with her life, made new friends and was earning her own money..."

"She wouldn't want him back," concluded Jay. "So, she rejects Keith, he gets angry and..."

"Kills her. And the cherry on top, with her dead, he gets sole ownership of the house."

Like a light bulb in a pitch-black room, Chris and Jay lit up with a new line of thinking. It propelled them to their feet, and they gathered up their case files, hastily shoving the results and reports into their arms before vanishing from the office.

With a mortified groan, I let my head rest on the desk, before gathering up the fractured pieces of my confidence and following them downstairs.

\* \* \*

As sheepish as I was for messing up the background search of the victim's address, I couldn't deny that Chris and Jay were the perfect pair when interviewing under pressure. The three of us sat at different points of the good-cop-bad-cop scale. I was good; kind and patient, usually. There was the odd occasion I lost my cool, like when talking to the infuriating Helena Brandon at the choir concert, but I chalked that up to a bad day. Jay sat more in the middle of the scale, able to go either way. And Chris, much like his usual personality outside of interviewing, held on to his moody and sour mood, no matter how guilty he thought the person to be.

By now, it was late afternoon and Keith Garrington was starting to look frayed by the prolonged stay in the custody suite. He eyed the two detectives opposite him with a tired, weary look, throwing glances at his legal aide with poorly concealed disdain. His pudgy unshaven face turned red under the stark LED lighting.

"What now?" he asked warily, watching Chris and Jay shuffle their papers like it was a trick or some sort of ruse.

Relegated to the observation room to watch from the bench, I knew I had a lot of making up to do before Chris would trust me in the interview room again.

"Just a few more questions," replied Jay, offering a coy grin. "When we spoke earlier, you were adamant that your relationship with Yvonne wasn't violent. However, we have records of three call-outs to your home address from concerned neighbours who could hear your arguments and were worried they were turning violent."

Keith Garrington sneered back, his muzzle like a growling dog's. "Nothing happened. The police never did anything, they just told us to keep it down and left. Prove there was violence. Prove I hurt Yvonne."

"Well, that's a bit hard to do since Yvonne isn't here anymore to advocate for herself."

"Exactly," sniffed Keith. "We argued, yeah. All the bloody time. But I never hit her."

An unexpected light hit me as the door to the observation room opened and a figure stood in the doorway. Aaron quickly closed it again, and without a word, he settled next to me, leaning against the desk that I sat on with my legs crossed.

"Ah, Chris is in there," he observed, looking at the interview through the small, one-way mirror. "Sending in the big guns."

"They found out about some old call-outs to the victim's address – domestic disturbances. He'll also get the house now that his ex-wife is dead," I explained. I kept my gaze on the interview; I couldn't let myself get distracted by Aaron when I'd already cocked up once for the day.

"Think it's enough to pin on him?"

I mulled over the question, tuning back into Jay and Chris talking. I couldn't be sure. As guilty as Keith Garrington looked – a contentious marriage, financial motivations, possible historic violence – I couldn't envision him copping to the crime. He was growing aggressive, but at the same time, he looked defeated. Hollow. Ever since I'd confirmed to him that Yvonne was really dead, he'd held himself like he was just a shell, ready to collapse inwardly at the slightest movement.

"We'll have to see."

Aaron shuffled next to me, putting his hands in his pockets but subtly moving an inch closer. I held still and focused on Jay.

"Domestic abuse isn't just physical violence," he was explaining, "it can be emotional, financial. Your neighbours were concerned enough about what they were hearing to call the police, so what were you arguing about?"

"It was bloody years ago, I can't remember."

"Try. The report says that your neighbours heard the sounds of screaming, crying, and objects smashing."

Keith's glare flickered between Chris and Jay. "Don't tell me you've never gotten into it with your missus. Shouted at each other, cried. Everyone argues."

"I've never hit my missus," Chris said flatly.

"Neither have I," Keith fired back.

Aaron shuffled again. "He's starting to look angry." He kept glancing at me out the corner of his eye, as though he was waiting for some sort of reaction.

"What is it?" I asked. I wasn't in the mood to be scrutinised and made that clear with a discontented scowl.

"You sure you're all right working on this case?"

"Of course, I am," I replied with a sniff. "Why wouldn't I be?"

Aaron turned his attention back to the interview, careful not to give anything else away, except for a thoughtful purse of his lips. "Well, you know… Sam."

At the mention of that name, my mind whirled, taking me far away from the present I faced, from the interview and the case. An intense feeling rose inside me, keen to ripple any calm. It was hatred, dread, and a mixture of every other unwanted emotion I had ever felt. It was my teenage naivety, leading me down a dark and unwanted path. His name invoked something inside me that I kept firmly hidden away from everyone in my life; a part of my past I pretended never happened.

I dragged myself back to the room. I couldn't get lost now, not when there was an urgent job to do. A woman was dead. My past wouldn't help me solve the case, it would only distract me and make me doubt myself. I would be quite content to never hear the name Sam Kingsley again in my life, and to forget the man ever existed.

"You think I can't handle being on a case involving domestic abuse?"

In the meantime, in the interview room, Chris leaned forwards across the table, subtly pressing harder. "So how do you explain the tip-off we received that you were spotted outside Yvonne's house on the night of her murder?"

Keith Garrington's hands trembled on the tabletop. "What? I was never there. I already told you."

"You can't explain your whereabouts for that night."

"I didn't kill her!"

Beside me, Aaron tensed up. "I never said that."

"You're thinking it," I hissed back. "I've worked plenty of cases involving DV; it's never been an issue before, and it won't be now." I watched him, waiting for some sort of hint of what he was thinking. He knew more than he was letting on, more than I'd ever told him. Somehow, Aaron had connected the dots.

"I know, Anna," he said quickly. "I'm just checking you're okay."

"Why wouldn't I be okay?"

"Because it's personal. And now, I know you better than before. Now we're... closer."

"You mean we're shagging?"

"It's more than that."

"Is it?" I asked. "It's been three months, Aaron, and the only part of our relationship that's different is that you left your toothbrush at my house."

He opened his mouth, but before any words made it out, Keith Garrington flew to his feet, smacking his hands on the tabletop hard enough to make the mirror shudder. Chris and Jay hadn't moved, although from their eerie stillness, I guessed they were as surprised by the outburst as I was. The duty solicitor scurried backwards, keen to get out of any firing line.

"I know where I was Saturday night. I was at a lock-in at The Bell Inn in Cawston. You can ask anyone there. I didn't kill Yvonne!"

And just like that, our prime suspect went out the window.

# Chapter Nine

I remained in the bad books for the rest of the day, although I consoled myself by thinking it wasn't entirely my fault and that Keith Garrington's last-minute alibi was actually the reason for everyone's foul mood. It was at least partly true, and by the time I left the station that night, it was far too late to do anything other than crawl into bed. The others had all retired earlier to the pub, to drown their sorrows in a night of bitching. I declined to join them.

The next day, Jay and Chris were more determined than ever to get Keith Garrington back into custody after his release. They elected to go to The Bell Inn, in the village of Cawston, a few miles from Aylsham, to suss out his alibi themselves, leaving me with the simple instruction of 'Don't fuck anything up', and to track down whoever made the anonymous tip-off supposedly placing Keith at the scene.

As soon as Maddie arrived, we set off for the community hall at St Mary's Church, where on Friday mornings they hosted a toddler dance class. Judging by the full car park, it was a popular one. Maddie and I had to park further down Nelson Avenue and walk up to the hall, but doing so gave us a chance to check on Yvonne's house. All was silent and undisturbed; it looked like Keith Garrington hadn't tried to gain access again.

"Well, you look like a wet weekend." Maddie had that look in her eye, one that told me she was searching for something juicy.

"What are you, seventy years old?" I snapped back. "My nanna used to say that phrase."

"Then your nanna had a good point, you do look thoroughly miserable. What's up?"

As much as I tried to stop myself, I sighed with discontent. I was just annoyed with my own ineptitude, Aaron's refusal to discuss moving forward and, mostly, the lack of progress. On top of all that, Aaron had brought up Sam, so along with my own self-pity, I now had a stream of unwanted memories floating around my head.

"Aaron's fucked up again, hasn't he?" said Maddie, reading my mind.

"What makes you think that?"

"Your frostiness and the fact that he told me last night at the pub."

I rolled my eyes. I knew Aaron and Maddie were good friends and had been for years, but her face practically danced with delight at the prospect of good gossip.

"What did he tell you?"

"Not much," she replied. "Chris and Jay were there so he couldn't say much."

"He was questioning whether I could work on this case."

Maddie scrunched her face into a frown. "Why?"

"Because it's in the tiniest conceivable way similar to an old *incident* of mine."

The email from Simon Hartley was still sitting in my inbox, unread. It didn't matter how many flags, exclamation points, or follow-up messages he sent, I would continue to ignore it. I didn't care what the Victim Support team had to say.

"Those darn men," Maddie said, rolling her eyes at me, "being all considerate and shit. How dare they."

"All right, point taken," I replied, surrendering before Maddie asked any more about the incident. "He probably meant it in a caring way. It just came across as questioning my ability."

"Just become a lesbian, Anna." Maddie shrugged her shoulders and held her hands up. "It's so much easier than dealing with *guys* and their awkwardness, and inability to connect to their feelings."

I paused as we reached the door to the community centre, letting out a small laugh. Maddie relaxed and a triumphant grin settled on her face.

The dance class was in full swing when I let myself into the community centre with Maddie right behind me. I noticed a new display in the foyer; photos of the choir concert Jay and I had attended and a collage of shots from the rehearsals. Yvonne was absent from all of them. I found that desperately sad; by all accounts, Yvonne had found a new lease of life with this group and now they were pretending she didn't exist, cutting her out of their history entirely. It seemed a strange way to mourn someone apparently so bubbly and well-loved.

In the main hall, brightly coloured ribbons littered the floor, threatening to trip anyone not paying enough attention. Small children raced back and forth, while adults sat around the edge of the hall and drank cups of tea, keeping a watchful eye on the carnage led by the enthusiastic dance teacher. On the opposite wall, a hatch to a small kitchen was open and two people bustled inside, the clangs of ceramic barely audible over the delighted screams of the toddlers. I recognised both the figures in the kitchen as I picked my way through the hall.

When I reached the hatch, Helena Brandon greeted me like a visitor, with a wide, insincere smile on her face and a cloth in hand. That was until a moment later, when she recognised me and the smile dropped.

"What do you want?" Her hostility stood out like a blaring siren among the happy chattering of the children and their parents.

A few little ones stopped playing and turned, looking at Maddie with wide eyes. She knelt down to greet them and soon the dancing was abandoned in favour of interacting with the cool police officer wearing the stab vest.

The second person in the kitchen turned around at Helena's brusque tone.

"Ah, Detective McArthur," Reverend Harding greeted me, abandoning the washing-up to appear at Helena's side. "Welcome. We are always happy to see new faces at our groups." He glanced around me to Maddie and her gang of tots.

"Even those in uniform." Helena sneered at the spectacle.

"I'm afraid I'm only here in a professional sense," I said, just as two little ones ran up to me and crashed into my legs. With a giggle and a wobble, they set off again, racing back across the hall whilst screaming nee-naw.

"You don't have any children?" the reverend asked me.

Next to him, Helena Brandon scoffed at his overt friendliness, and I couldn't help but match her expression at the personal question.

"Not yet," I said.

This was exactly the sort of group my mother was desperate for me to have children for, so she could be the doting grandma and take the baby to. This toddler group was as much for socialising for the parents and carers as it was for the kids to supposedly learn how to dance. Unfortunately for her, children were not on my agenda yet.

"I'm here to ask some more questions, if that's okay." I glanced around the room, where everything was merry as the dance teacher resumed prancing across the dancefloor and a few of the children begged Maddie to join in. "Now seems to be a good time."

"Actually, it's not," said Helena Brandon. "We're very busy."

"This will only take a few minutes."

Helena opened her mouth again, but Reverend Harding silenced her by placing a hand on her shoulder, which he hastily withdrew when she turned her nettled glare on him.

"We can spare a few minutes for the police," he said delicately. "After all, Yvonne used to help us at this very group. What can we help you with, Detective?"

"Well, it's about these groups, actually," I said, getting in quick before Helena Brandon changed her mind. "I need a list of everyone present at the choir rehearsal on Saturday night. The night Yvonne was killed."

"What for?" she demanded.

"For our inquiries," I replied simply.

Reverend Harding scratched his chin. "I can get that. Let me pop to the office."

He scurried off through a door at the back of the kitchen, leaving Helena scowling at me. Behind me, I could hear the dance teacher desperately trying to regain the attention of the two-year-olds.

"Did you see anything unusual when you left the rehearsal on Saturday night?" I asked.

Helena scoffed at me as she turned up her nose. "Like what?"

"A different car on the street, someone walking about at that time of night. We've had a report of someone in the area, but we need to establish who saw them and when."

"Oh?" said Helena Brandon. Her eyes, a beautiful green colour, flashed devilishly at me and her lips curled into a smirk. "So you finally have an idea of who could do such a horrible thing? Better late than never, I suppose. At least now you can get back to catching the murderer rather than harassing innocent boys hanging out with their friends."

"I'm sorry?" I gave Helena Brandon a hard stare. The last time I met her with Jay, she had been bristly and sharp but now she wasted no time in jumping into antagonism.

I glimpsed a look of displeasure on her face which disappeared as quickly as it came. "Jacob told me you turned up when he was out with his friends the other day. I shouldn't have to remind you that my son is underage and you cannot question him without a parent present."

"I didn't question your son," I said defensively. "I asked some questions to his group of friends, some of whom were likely to have been in the area when Yvonne Garrington was killed."

Helena Brandon huffed at me and folded her arms as she attempted to stare me down. It had been a long time since I had been squared up to, but it still sent the same shiver down my back. My sixth sense for knowing when things were getting dangerously tense hadn't lessened over the years behind a desk. I wasn't about to let this woman see she could intimidate me, however.

"Regardless of your excuses," said Helena and she dropped her voice low, "if you ever approach my son regarding this investigation again, you will have me and my solicitor to answer to."

I swallowed hard. "You and your solicitor could be seen as obstructing a police officer if you refuse to cooperate with our investigation."

Around us, the hall fell quiet, although it was impossible to silence toddlers. I felt a dozen eyes on me as tension filled the air, all the adults around us could sense there was something going on and children wondering what the lull was. Helena Brandon continued to glower at me, but I was not about to let her glare her way out of answering my questions.

Reverend Harding reappeared at the kitchen door. He read the situation in a split second and jumped between us.

"Now, now," he said, guiding Helena away into the recess of the kitchen. "Let's not bring these difficult feelings into such an innocent setting. Here you go, Detective McArthur. If you have any further questions for us, Helena and I would be happy to talk to you after the group is finished."

"With my solicitor," Helena finished.

Unable to help myself, I gave a dissatisfied grumble and folded up the paper handed to me by Harding. "That won't be necessary. If we need any further information from you, I'll be sure to ask you to the station."

With little other choice, I spun round on my heels and exited the community centre, leaving the happy lilts of the toddlers and the piercing glare of Helena Brandon behind. After a hasty goodbye to the toddlers, Maddie appeared at my side.

"What a bitch," she said, looking back in the direction of Helena Brandon with a firm scowl, before she caught herself. "I mean, what a shame she wasn't more cooperative."

I harrumphed in agreement, still tasting the bitterness that the interaction had left behind in my mouth. "My question is, why."

\* \* \*

Back at the station, Maddie and I set about calling the list of choir members and helpers in an attempt to track down the source of the anonymous tip-off. If someone was able to place Keith Garrington at the scene of his ex-wife's murder and to disprove his alibi, we needed to find them. I was keen not to let Helena Brandon's hostility irritate me any longer, although I couldn't shake the nagging feeling that came with wanting to know why. It was as if merely talking to a police officer was enough to rile her up.

Just after ending another unfruitful call, my desk phone rang with the shrill noise that signalled an internal call from somewhere in the building. I picked it up and the exasperated front-desk officer informed me there was a visitor demanding to see a member of the Serious Crimes team. She had given her name as AJ Masters.

I jumped to my feet, startling Maddie in the process.

"Exciting development?" she asked, giggling at my enthusiasm.

"Alyssa-June Masters just turned up downstairs. Trust Jay and Chris to be otherwise engaged when something like this happens out of the blue. Come on, this could be what we've been waiting for."

"Well, should we call them?"

"No way," I said, already heading downstairs. "I can handle this on my own."

What I didn't say out loud to Maddie was that I needed this opportunity to prove to both Chris and Jay that I wasn't useless. I needed to make up for missing the disturbance call-outs to the Garrington house.

In the front lobby, a throng of people faced us, the usual bustle of the police station on a weekday morning. Across the way, sitting on the furthest set of uncomfortable chairs, I spotted a sun-kissed young blonde woman with a paler, slightly older woman who had to be her mother. The younger one looked like she had come straight from the airport; she had sunglasses on her head and her tiny orange shorts were quite out of season for a late-September day in Norfolk.

As I passed by, I nodded to the desk officer and he held up three fingers to me like a Girl Scout pledge – Interview Room 3 was free for me to use. Perfect.

I made my way over with Maddie still by my side. The mother nudged her daughter as I approached, and the two of them stood up to greet us.

"Alyssa-June?" I asked and held out my hand to shake the young woman's. She trembled at my touch. "I'm Detective Constable Anna McArthur. This is my colleague, PC Maddie Greene. I understand you wanted to talk to someone about the death of Yvonne Garrington."

"Is he here?" she asked urgently. She was tall and slender, her blonde hair falling in perfect beach waves around her shoulders. I could see how she'd turned Keith Garrington's head.

"Who?"

"Keith," she said. "Is he here, do you have him locked up?"

"Um, no," I replied. "Keith Garrington was questioned but released pending investigation. We're still investigating his ex-wife's—"

"You need to arrest him!" AJ said, her voice rising above the thrum of the station. "You need to arrest him now. He killed his wife!"

## Chapter Ten

AJ spoke like someone had placed her on fast forward. I marvelled at how she barely stopped for breath, ranting on and on about the moment she heard that Yvonne Garrington had died and she *knew* it was Keith. Even as Maddie, just as unable to get a word in edgewise as me, tried to usher AJ to Interview Room 3, she still carried on, eyes wide and mouth running constantly, like an engine. Her mother, who quietly introduced herself as Carolyn Masters, trudged along behind, apparently used to AJ's non-stop nature.

I managed to stop AJ long enough for Maddie to set the recording equipment up and for us to take all necessary details before we began. But every second she held her tongue, I could see AJ growing more and more agitated, desperate to get the words out.

"All right," I said as I settled myself down. "So, Alyssa-June."

"Call me AJ," she said. She tapped her long, shocking pink nails on the tabletop. Next to her, her mother bit down on her thumb.

"Okay, AJ." I took a deep breath. "You said Keith Garrington killed his wife – that's a very strong accusation. Do you have any evidence that he committed murder?"

"No," said AJ, "but as soon as I heard that his wife had been killed, I knew it was him. He always said he wished she was dead, that it would make his divorce and life so much easier."

"So, just to confirm, you don't have any proof that Keith killed Yvonne?"

AJ gave a dramatic sigh and flicked her long hair over her tanned shoulder. "I didn't see it happen, no. I was in Spain! But I've spent enough time with the man this last year to know he's capable of it. He was, like, bitter about it all – about his divorce. When things started to go to shit, he blamed her for it. He hated her. Like, I know hate is a strong word, but this was stronger. They really hated each other. There were intense, strong feelings left over from when they were married, and Keith wasn't interested in dealing with that or working through it. I suggested therapy, or spiritual healing, but he said that was bullshit."

When she paused for breath, I seized the opportunity to jump in. "Did Keith plan to kill Yvonne? Did he share any ideas with you, describe ways he would kill her?"

"No." AJ looked appalled by this. "Not that I knew. But, look, I just know he did it. There isn't anyone else. Keith may seem like a nice man on the surface, but I've spent months with him. Trust me, he's not. I may not have *evidence* or proof he did it, but I know in my gut. You don't spend months with someone without discovering their true self. Keith's energy was always caught up in hating Yvonne, it was only a matter of time before that energy needed to come out somehow."

This wasn't going anywhere. I shared a glance with Maddie, but she looked as bewildered as I felt. As much as I believed in gut feelings and just *knowing* some things, there hadn't yet been a murder conviction based on such a flimsy case.

"All right, let's start at the beginning." I decided that maybe more specific questions would help AJ remain focused. "From what I've learned so far, Keith left Yvonne last year to be with you and the two of you ran off to Spain together. Is that correct?"

"Yeah."

"So, at what point did you realise he resented Yvonne enough to want to cause her harm?"

AJ tapped her chin with one of her long fingernails and glanced at her mother. "About three months in, when we started to run out of money. He'd get very angry, would rant and rave and blame Yvonne for everything, even though he hadn't spoken to her in months. When the divorce was finalised, it only got worse."

"In what way did it get worse?"

"Like, just worse! He'd lose his temper more often, nearly every day, it never stopped. He wanted life to be like a paradise, but it all turned to hell. I guess, he resented that it all went that way. His energy just grew more and more negative as time went on."

"How did your relationship end?" I asked.

AJ glanced at her mother again. Carolyn watched the conversation between me and AJ with wary eyes, still biting her thumbnail. She seemed too nervous to catch her daughter's subtle glint and the way she hitched her breath.

"I ended it," AJ said. "I was sick of his moaning, his grouchiness. Spain was heaven and he was ruining it. It was never serious anyway, neither of us wanted to get married or anything. We were just having fun."

"It doesn't sound to me like Keith Garrington was a lot of fun," I replied.

AJ shrugged. "He was, to begin with. I guess I need someone more my own age. I still like to party all night and sleep all day. You know what I mean?"

She thrust her hand at me, waiting for my reply, and out the corner of my eye, I caught Maddie's face contort as she suppressed a laugh. I didn't know what she was sniggering about; I was closer to AJ's age than I was to Maddie's. Although Maddie was much more of a young spirit, and out of the two of us, she was more likely to be partying all night than me.

"How did Keith take you breaking off your relationship?"

AJ looked at Carolyn again. "I don't know. I just kind of left. I packed my bags one day and headed for town."

I gave AJ a surprised scowl. "You did a midnight flit?"

"No, no, I didn't. I left him a note."

"You broke up with him with a note?"

"I…" AJ trailed off.

To my surprise, she seemed to lose her words – a first time for everything, I guessed. But once again, she looked towards her mum. Carolyn was glancing between us all, but she didn't seem to be really *seeing* her daughter. She didn't catch her nervous glances. There was something unspoken between them and it was hindering this interview.

I leant across the table. "Mrs Masters, are you okay?" I asked her.

The woman was startled by my question. "Yes. Of course, I am. Why?"

"You look a little peaky," I said. I gave Maddie a subtle nudge with my elbow. "Maddie, do you mind taking Mrs Masters to get some water?"

"Oh yeah," Maddie said, catching my drift, and she peered closely at Carolyn Masters' face. "You do look a little pale. Let's get some water."

Before she had a chance to refuse, Maddie ushered Carolyn Masters to her feet and over to the door. My colleague gave me a wink as she left the interview room and it took all my strength not to wink back.

The slam of the door only managed to heighten AJ's jitters. With her mother out of the room, she regarded me with a suspicious gaze.

"Okay," I said with a deep breath, leaning forward on the table. "It's just you and me now. There's no need to hide whatever it is you don't want your mum to know about your relationship with Keith Garrington."

"What makes you think I'm hiding something?" She stiffened, her pink nails tapping rapidly on the side of the table.

"Well, you came straight to the police station from the airport for a reason. Something made you want to come back to the country. You tell me you believe Keith killed Yvonne but have no evidence to back up that claim… unless you actually do."

AJ's face paled a little. Her fingers tapped faster.

"AJ, now is the time to tell me. If Keith Garrington is a danger to anyone else, we need to know."

"It only happened once." Her voice was small, like a mouse.

"What happened once?" I asked.

"It… you know. He lost control."

Like a sinking ship, my stomach dropped. I knew what she meant; I knew her expression and her nervousness, better than most.

I inhaled deeply. "Ah. He was violent towards you."

"Like I said, just once," said AJ, sitting up to match my posture as if copying me might help her shame. "I didn't let him do it again; after that, I was gone. But we used to argue like hell. He was so bitter over Yvonne. Sometimes I even found it fun to wind him up, do and say things that I knew would remind him of her. But the temper, the violence... it scared me."

I nodded. I understood what AJ meant; the sudden change from thinking you know someone and their emotions, to being totally blindsided by their anger. The shock at the capacity they had to hurt.

"I know what you mean. And I'm guessing your mum doesn't know. You haven't told her that Keith hurt you?"

AJ shook her head, making her loose waves of hair tussle around her like a model from a shampoo advert. "She always thought I was naive and stupid for running off to Spain with him. I didn't want to prove her right."

Ah, parents. I wondered if there ever came an age where children stopped hiding things from their parents for fear of what they would think. I was almost thirty and I still had my secrets.

I cleared my throat, which made AJ meet my gaze. "Your mum loves you, that much is clear to me. Given the threat you think Keith poses, maybe telling your mum isn't a bad idea. Were the police involved during this incident?"

"No, I just got the hell out of there. I blocked Keith's number, took the money from the account and got the first bus I could. But you know what I mean, right? Feeling so ashamed that you would rather just forget about it all than remember it? I heard through friends that after I left, Keith came back to England. And then Mum told me that his ex-wife had been murdered and I panicked and thought, *what if he did it?* What if he lost it after I left and went back home and killed her? I don't know. I don't know what he's capable of. I just… can't let him hurt anyone else."

\* \* \*

"Busy?"

Aaron looked up from his computer screen, offering nothing more than a tight grimace at me as I poked my head into his office. AJ's recollection of what had transpired between her and Keith Garrington sparked something in my mind. Maddie was seeing AJ and her mother out so I seized the opportunity I had before Chris and Jay got back, because the longer I let it play on my mind, the worse it would become.

I let myself in and sat down opposite him. His office was warm, heated up by the bright midday sun, which helped to take the edge off. My hands found each other in my lap and my fingers twisted together.

"Simon Hartley contacted you, didn't he?"

Aaron didn't need to say anything to confirm that. I could tell he had by just the tiny twitch in the corner of his mouth.

"He's been trying to get in contact with you all week," he replied stiffly. "You've been ignoring him."

"I have a case to deal with," I said.

"This is important too."

It wasn't every day that I got an email from Victim Support, but I wasn't prepared to allocate it headspace at the moment. Because if I did, then I had to remember who I was all those years ago. But they had clearly got in contact with Aaron as well, given that he'd made the link between Sam Kingsley and me working on a case involving domestic violence. Now I needed to make it clear to him that I wasn't affected by this in any way.

"It's not important," I said.

A slow blink and slight twitch in the corner of his mouth again showed he didn't believe me.

"It isn't," I said. "They'll just want me to give a statement for the upcoming parole board hearing. I have nothing to say, nothing to contribute."

"Then why are you in here?"

I hated the smug little grin he gave me when I floundered for an answer. I could wipe that smile from his face if I wanted to, using some sort of womanly charm, but he had a good point. Why had I come to Aaron if I didn't want to talk about it?

"Because it's looking more and more likely that this case is involving an unhappy relationship and domestic violence. And I know more about those sorts of things than most people." I glanced down at my lap, my twisted fingers looking like a spider. "But I'm ninety-nine percent sure I never told you the whole story. So how do you know?"

"I don't," Aaron admitted, and thankfully, I saw a brief look of embarrassment. "I've pieced a few things together over the years. You have an ex-boyfriend who's been in prison for the last ten years for GBH. You were upfront about that when you joined the job. However, ten years is a hell of a sentence for a first conviction, so there must have been multiple convictions and the sentences stacked. And Victim Support wouldn't be contacting you unless you were also a victim somehow so…"

I sensed something hot prickle at the back of my neck, running up and down until my whole body was flushed with discomfort. I felt like I was eighteen again; naive, inexperienced, and madly in love with someone who had a hell of a temper on him. Sam was handsome and he knew it, with piercing blue eyes and a looming and lean physique. His nose and chin were angular, like they'd been chiselled from stone. His confidence drew me in and made up for the lack of my own, but it didn't take long before his true colours shone through. He made the wrong friends and the wrong choices, and soon the law caught up with him.

"Domestic violence is prevalent, Anna," Aaron said gently, pulling me from my thoughts. "You know this. There's no shame in what happened."

I wasn't like that now. I wasn't a meek pushover, too afraid to speak up. If anything, the events spurred me on until that teenager was just a distant memory and now I was determined not to let others hurt the same way that I had.

"The parole board isn't meeting until December," said Aaron, shuffling in his seat to get a better look at me. A cloud drifted over the sun, casting us into a deep shadow, so dark it took a moment for my eyes to adjust. "You have plenty of time to decide if you want to make a statement for them."

"I have nothing to say."

"Then say nothing." He gave a shrug but the firmness of his words showed that I was sounding more like the petulant teenager I used to be. "No one is going to make you. But what better way to show that you haven't let him ruin your life than to let him see how far you've come. A detective, helping victims and bringing perpetrators to justice. I don't know what you were like back then, but the Anna I know now wouldn't be scared to do something like this. The Anna I know is fearless."

\* \* \*

Chris and Jay were in a foul mood by the time they made it back to the office at the end of the day. After relaying to them what AJ Masters had disclosed about her time with Keith Garrington, they set about tracking him down, but just as we'd predicted, he was laying low again. Further to that, Keith's alibi about being at a lock-in at The Bell Inn pub had been confirmed by several of the other patrons. He may not have been back in the country long, but Keith Garrington had managed to find a few like-minded acquaintances to drink his free time away with.

"It must be a cover," Jay reasoned, leaning so far back in his chair I wondered if he was going to fall over. "They must be covering for him. He could've snuck out during the lock-in to murder Yvonne. Who's to say these friends of his aren't covering for him?"

"We just need one clue placing him at the scene," said Chris. He was pacing again. "One fingerprint, one hair. One reliable sighting. Something to confirm Keith has been back in that house since he left Yvonne. Where are we with the rest of the lab reports? Anything interesting come back?"

"Nothing yet," I replied. I was worried that more bad news would tip them both over the edge.

"What about the tip-off? Any luck tracking it down?" Jay asked.

I shook my head with regret and winced at the muffled swear words that followed.

Chris gritted his teeth and growled at no one in particular. "We were *this* close to having him. Everything points to Garrington so far – messy divorce, even messier finances, jealousy, history of domestic abuse. The statement by his ex-fling is useful but not enough. We need just one solid piece of evidence placing him at the scene."

"I could chase the lab… again," offered Jay. "One of the reports we're waiting for could be the answer to our prayers."

Chris shook his head. "Keep trying but we need to focus on the tip-off angle. Whoever reported it in is a key witness."

"But doesn't the anonymous tip-off feel a bit too convenient?" I asked. "Without it, we have nothing to say Keith Garrington had even been in contact with Yvonne. We've asked all the neighbours and Yvonne's church group, and no one saw him there that night. Where has it come from?"

"Who would want us to believe it was Keith Garrington, though?" Jay looked at Chris. "Maybe they saw someone who looked like Keith, but wasn't him."

"Or maybe they want to throw us off the trail by implicating Keith," I offered.

"Or maybe it's someone who knows his history with Yvonne, and they are scared of him," said Chris. "At least one of the neighbours knows he's capable of violence, someone used to call the police when they were arguing."

Jay nodded along knowingly while I couldn't help but roll my eyes. Something about the anonymous call didn't sit right with me and I couldn't shake the feeling that instead of helping the case, it was muddying the waters. If someone had really seen Keith at the scene on the night of the murder, why not just say it directly? If they were scared of him, we could offer protection. Instead, we were relying on info given to us by someone whose intentions were unknown. Someone who could've wanted to push our attention in a certain direction.

"What's our next steps?" asked Jay, stifling a yawn. That set off Chris, who yawned loud enough to shake the windows.

"We need to find Keith Garrington," Chris replied simply. "We've got every copper in Norfolk on the lookout so chances are he'll be found over the weekend. Keep your phones on, I guarantee we'll be called in at some point and we'll take it from there."

"And what if it isn't him?" I asked. I hated the thought of putting all our eggs in one basket. We could be so focused on Keith Garrington that the real murderer was walking free right under our noses.

Chris let out the tiniest of frustrated groans before catching himself. He gave me a sidelong glance, one that told me he was fed up with my questions, and settled his gaze on Jay.

"I know you want to believe there is more to this, Anna, but sometimes there just isn't."

Managing to look a little more sheepish than Chris did, Jay turned to me. "Yeah. Sometimes the most obvious suspect is the culprit. The evidence points to them for a reason. We had a bad feeling about this guy since the start and nothing has disproven that. It's very likely he did it, Anna."

"But there's always a chance–" I said.

"Drop it, Anna." Chris finally stopped pacing, falling into his chair with the sigh of someone twenty years older than himself. "Not every case has a genius mastermind or a cunning killer. Sometimes they are just open and shut. Nothing glamourous or exciting about them."

So as not to risk pissing them off even more, I decided it was best to close my mouth.

## Chapter Eleven

The next morning, I powered my way down Nelson Avenue with an uneasy feeling of déjà vu steadily wiping away my tiredness. A police presence filled the street once again, crime-scene tape and forensic vans disturbing the Saturday morning peace. I thought back to what I'd left behind in my warm flat; Aaron still asleep and the cat happily curled up by his feet. We'd just watched TV in silence and gone to bed the previous evening, like a strange old married couple who no longer had anything worth saying to each other. Although I was grateful he was there, I absolutely didn't want to talk about the embarrassing admission I had made to him about my past.

And then Jay called and woke me up, sounding just as groggy as I felt, and insisted I went to Nelson Avenue. So here I was.

"It's Saturday," I said to him as I approached. Yvonne Garrington's house was the focus of the commotion again and white-clad SOCOs traipsed in and out of the front door. I was expecting a call into work at some point that weekend – Keith Garrington couldn't stay invisible forever – but I wasn't expecting it so early.

Jay yawned loudly and folded his arms as he leaned against the crumbly garden wall of Churchside Cottages. "Trust me, I know," he replied. "But we needed you for this."

"What's happened?"

He looked towards the house, his face filling with confusion and remorse. "Let's just wait for Chris before we go in. Early this morning, next door" – he pointed to the Welles household – "reported hearing noises from the house and called 999. Officers attended and found Keith inside."

Jay's explanation didn't include a conclusion to the story. But the scene-of-crime officers only attended when the danger was over and there was forensic work to be done, so it didn't take me too long to figure out what they'd found inside.

"We think it was an overdose," said Jay sadly. "He was on Yvonne's bed."

"Oh God."

Chris swaggered up to us. Surprisingly, he didn't look as irritated at the early-morning wake-up call as I expected him to be. He read the mood in a split second.

"I know what you're thinking," he said to Jay. "That we pushed him too far. We didn't. We weren't to know he would do something like this."

"He was our number one suspect in his wife's death," Jay replied, with a shrug of his shoulders. "We shouldn't have let him go."

"*Ex*-wife. And we weren't to know what he was planning."

"Why do you think he killed himself?" I asked. Clearly Chris had spent more time thinking this over than Jay and I had.

Chris drew in a stiff breath. "Grief or guilt. If it was a reaction to killing Yvonne then I would've expected him to do it right away, not almost a week later. Why would he wait until now to do it?" Reaching out and clicking his fingers, he caught the attention of the nearest SOCO. "Have you found a suicide note yet?"

The SOCO still had their mask on, meaning only their eyes were showing, but they shook their head. "No note. There's nothing like that inside."

"Then our investigation continues," said Chris, turning back to Jay and me. "Until we can be certain he killed Yvonne, we'll keep going."

"But yesterday you were sure it was him," I pointed out.

Chris shrugged. "I was thinking over what you said. Keith Garrington certainly looks guilty from the outside, but the evidence isn't so clear-cut. And, as you said, that anonymous call was just a bit too convenient."

I felt renewed and secretly a little bit pleased by Chris's words, but Jay didn't look convinced, though he nodded nonetheless. With slow shuffles, all three of us made our way into the house. The SOCOs had now left the upstairs and I supposed there wasn't much else for them to examine. Following Chris, we made our way towards Yvonne's bedroom. As the guys peeked inside the wide-open door first, I took my chance to check the other rooms since last time I was here I'd only seen the blood-soaked kitchen.

There was nothing remarkable in the bathroom; it was clean and tidy, with none of the mould that lined mine at home. All the usual stuff was there, including some mid-range bath products and salts; it looked like Yvonne liked to pamper herself once in a while.

The second bedroom held nothing of note, it was just Yvonne's wardrobe room with sensible middle-aged fashion and quite a lot of shoes. Everywhere in the house was neat and well-cared for. I wondered if she had decorated since Keith left; a fresh new start for the house and for her.

Although Jay and Chris were still in the doorway, I peered into the master bedroom next, finding it exactly how I expected – clean and tidy like the rest of Yvonne's house. Yvonne wasn't one to leave discarded clothes on the floor. She had a nightstand with a lamp and a dog-eared romance novel. On the other side, another nightstand had a phone charger cable and a box of condoms. Strange things to leave on the opposite side of the bed, unless you had someone else in the bed too. Seemed that Yvonne had had company since her divorce from Keith.

It was hard to ignore the obvious in the room and eventually I let myself look. The rotund figure of Keith Garrington was lying on the bed, on the side that must have been his at one point. He looked comfortable, and if it hadn't been for the mess of blister packs strewn across the bed, he could have been mistaken for sleeping. But there was no movement, no gentle rising and falling of his chest or flicker of his eyes. He was gone.

His face wasn't peaceful, as most people expect the dead to be. It was warped and contorted with pain, his gaze locked in a far-off stare.

He was still racked with grief.

\* \* \*

I was set to work by Chris to establish a time frame for Keith Garrington's last hours and what he had done inside the house. Jay went next door to interview the Welleses whilst Chris spoke to the lead forensic investigator. I knew I had been purposely left in the house because it was the least desirable of all the jobs. I wanted to get out, it still stank of blood and now oozed sadness from every wall.

After half an hour, I managed to sneak out the back door, where a blanket of autumn leaves covered the small garden. A garden gate at the back joined onto an alleyway that also led to the garden of Robert and Sue Welles, and reemerged onto the road beside their property. I followed it, relieved to see that when I arrived, I was outside the crime-scene cordon, and nodded nonchalantly to the officer guarding the alleyway. He nodded back.

I started the short walk down the road, heading for the community centre; I could hear the soft music drifting from the church. The crime scene hadn't stopped some sort of service from taking place. I contemplated going inside, but decided that if Helena Brandon was in there, then I was better off waiting for it to finish, when it would be easier to catch Reverend Harding or any other members of the congregation alone.

Being careful to stay out of sight of Chris or Jay down the street, I fought my way through the overgrowth at the back of the community centre.

If anyone knew any information about Keith Garrington's appearance at Yvonne's house, it might just be Bos.

The bushes and trees muffled out the haunting organ music, but I heard no cackling teen laughter or chatter as I approached the hideout. When I emerged, picking pieces of hedge from my hair, I found it empty, apart from Jacob Brandon who was lounging across the sofa.

"Oh shit!" he said, jumping to his feet at the sight of me. "What are you doing here?"

"I'm looking for Bos," I said.

Jacob hastily stuffed something behind his back, out of my sight, but the telltale smell of cigarette smoke was undeniable. He was flirting with danger, smoking so close to the church his parents were leaders of.

"Well, he's not here," Jacob said with the same tone of indignation as his mother. "I'll tell him you came by later."

The lad seemed unusually jittery. I wondered if it had something to do with my last unannounced visit and his mother's fury, or if it was just because I had caught him smoking.

"Where is he?"

Jacob shrugged. "I don't know. He disappears during the day. But he's not here."

"Jacob," I said calmly. "You seem a bit nervous. I'm not fussed you're smoking back here. I just want to talk to Bos or anyone who might be able to help answer some questions about the incident down the road." I thumbed back in the direction of Yvonne's house. Even here in the hideout, the organ music from the church and distant chatter of the police officers penetrated enough to be noticeable.

With a shuffle of his feet, Jacob gave me a glare. "I'm not talking to you. You're police. You took our drink last time you were here."

"Yeah, well," – I rolled my shoulders – "you told your mother about my little visit. How about I don't mention the fags to her, and you don't tell her I was here. Deal?"

After a moment to scrutinise whether I was being sincere or not, Jacob shrugged once again and sat himself back down on the creaking sofa. It appeared he wanted to take our deal as he gave up hiding the cigarette behind his back.

"Mum doesn't know I'm here," he said, his jitters fading away as he took a long drag. "She thinks I'm at home, doing my homework. She said if I hang out with Bos again, she'll ground me."

"Where are your parents?"

"In the church, helping Reverend Harding prepare for tomorrow night."

"What's happening tomorrow night?"

"Nothing," he said quickly.

"Oh well…" It looked like I was going to have to try harder to get anything useful out of Jacob today. "I won't tell your mum you're here. Just tell me where Bos is and I'll get out of your way."

Jacob gave me a disbelieving look. "She'll still find out. She always knows what I'm doing. It's like she has a sixth sense or something."

I mulled over Jacob's words. I remembered being a teenager, wanting to go out and try new things but having the constant scrutiny of my parents on my back. Some might say that was what drove me to keep company with someone like Sam, to spite my parents and exercise my teenage rebellion. Helena Brandon struck me as an excruciatingly overbearing parent and there were plenty of tricks overbearing parents could use to keep an eye on their children.

"Did you know," I said to Jacob, making my way to lean on the tower of pallets, upwind of the smoke, "that some parents use an app on their child's mobile phone to keep track of them?"

Jacob sat up and patted his pocket, pulling out his phone.

"I'm not saying that's what your mum is doing. But I've seen it used before, it can be quite useful for keeping track of lying teens."

"Really?" Jacob now frowned at his phone screen. "What's it called?"

"I don't know, it'll be somewhere in the hidden files on your phone. They don't make these apps obvious. So, anyway, where are Bos and your other friends?"

Jacob continued to scowl at his mobile phone, but he hummed at me nonetheless. "Bos'll be back soon, he probably walked to town to find some food. The others aren't about yet, it's too early. Why?"

"I just wanted to know if anyone had remembered anything about Yvonne Garrington's death," I replied. "I'll swing by Bos's house on my way back, he might be there."

I still remembered the lad's address from my days on the beat. I had dropped him back home after catching him out up to no good more times than I could count over the years.

Jacob snorted. "You'll be lucky. His mum kicked him out two months ago."

"Oh really? Then where is he staying?"

Jacob gestured around him. "Here. He's been sleeping in the den all summer. We don't mention it, Bos gets a bit arsy when you talk about it. His mum only kicked him out cos he wasn't getting along with her new boyfriend."

"Ah." I felt a strange new sensation overtake me, something I hadn't ever felt for Bos – sympathy. The gobby little shite had a rough home life, I knew that, but I had no idea he was now homeless.

Luckily, Jacob was still engrossed in his phone, searching for the spying app. He didn't notice my little slip of surprise.

"All right," I said decisively. "Well, when you see him, tell him Officer McArthur is looking for him."

"Will do," Jacob mumbled back, then waved me away.

"And stay out of trouble, Jacob."

He snorted. "It's you who needs to stay out of trouble. My mum can be a right dragon and she's got it in for you."

"Oh really? And why's that?"

"She doesn't like it when people stick their noses where they don't belong." His gaze didn't leave his phone but Jacob's hollow words sent a shiver through me.

"Not very Christian of her," I remarked. "We're trying to solve a murder here. Why doesn't she want to cooperate?"

Jacob shrugged back, his attention back on the screen. "Dunno. I'm just warning you."

"I'll bear that in mind," I said.

I left the hideout, happy to sneak back to the house and avoid Helena Brandon's wrath, although I couldn't ignore the curiosity that piqued as I wondered why she was so against us.

## Chapter Twelve

After finishing off the morning in the oppressive terraced house, I picked up coffees and sandwiches from a cafe in town and headed back to the station, hoping the offering of lunch would help pick us up after a difficult start to the day. I found Chris and Jay in the Serious Crimes office, still wearing the same expressions of regret at the situation. Their faces lit up when they saw I came bearing gifts.

"You didn't have to buy lunch," Jay said but he immediately took a large bite of his bacon sarnie.

"Don't get used to it," I said. "I can't afford lunch all round much on my salary. Have any luck speaking with the neighbours?"

Chris shook his head as he tentatively sniffed the coffee on offer. "No. Keith was more careful this time, no one noticed him entering the property. His car was a street away. How did you get on with his last steps?"

"Same," I replied, "not much luck with any of it. All evidence suggests he broke into the house via the front door, touched or moved nothing, then went upstairs. He brought the pills with him. The noise the neighbours heard must've been him choking or thrashing around."

"A sad turn of events," Chris mumbled under his breath.

"I noticed Yvonne had had a house guest," I said just as Jay dropped a piece of bacon onto his desk. "There's a box of condoms on the side, and a phone charger on the wrong side of the bed. Did any of the neighbours mention Yvonne having someone stay over?"

"I noticed that too," said Jay. "I asked the neighbours about it, but none of them said they'd seen anyone staying at Yvonne's. Not all night anyway. She had people pop by, as you do."

Chris shrugged. "Doesn't need to be a sleepover to use that box of condoms."

"Good point," replied Jay.

"But by all accounts, Yvonne was now a firm part of the church group."

I huffed as I landed in my chair and unfolded my chicken mayo sandwich. Jay polished off the last of his bacon sandwich, and Chris had stopped eating to give me a look, urging me to explain further.

"Over the last year," I said, "Yvonne had got very close to those in the church group. Neighbours are friendly but they aren't always home or paying attention. Yvonne talked to the church group. I find it hard to believe none of them knew of any relationships Yvonne might have started, or any *close* friendships she might have developed."

"If she was seeing someone, then no one had noticed. That doesn't mean that there wasn't someone in Yvonne's life, just that they were being very discreet about it," concluded Chris as he returned to his sandwich.

I took it to mean he was quietly entertaining my line of thinking.

"Why were they being so discreet about it?" I said, although from the look that Chris gave me, I knew speculating on that point was pointless. There were simply too many possibilities.

"And how did she keep it a secret?" said Jay. "Those are some very close neighbours. Surely they must have noticed someone popping by, even just for an hour or two."

For a second, I swear I saw Chris glance at me. "You'd be surprised how easy it is to keep something like that a secret from those you see every day."

Jay didn't notice his look, but he sniggered into his coffee cup. "Speaking from experience, hey? Do you have a secret lover you're hiding from us?"

Chris shook his head. "Not me. Happily married and one woman is enough. But you never know…"

And again, he looked towards me, this time causing a shiver of paranoia to zap down my neck. I broke his gaze, looking away before my sense of dread gave something away. Did Chris know? He couldn't, I would never tell him. And Aaron was even more secretive than me. But still, he was an astute man and he knew Aaron well enough to know when there was something he was hiding…

Time to change the topic.

"I tried to reach out to Brady Boston again," I said. "Word on the street is that he's living in the den behind the community centre at the moment, after being kicked out by his mum. If anyone heard anything happen the night Yvonne died, it would be him."

"Where did you hear that?" Jay asked through another mouthful.

"Jacob Brandon told me."

Jay stuttered, choking as he swallowed hastily. "You spoke to Jacob Brandon again? Didn't his mum make it clear to you and Maddie yesterday that she doesn't want us speaking to him without a parent present?"

"I didn't go looking for him," I replied defensively. "I just ran into him whilst looking for Bos."

Chris considered this. "Jay's right, you shouldn't have spoken to him. He is underage, after all."

"We didn't even talk about the investigation." I felt my hackles rise. So much for easing the tension in the team. "I just asked him where I could find Bos and he told me Bos has been sleeping in the den. That was all."

Both of the guys fell quiet, suddenly very interested in their lunches. However, I caught them looking at one another, one of their glances that they understood without having to say a word.

"All right," said Chris, after a pause. "I guess we'll just have to see how that goes. Next time, consult us before you go off-task."

In terms of a telling-off from Chris, that was a mild one.

"Yes, boss," I said, and let my defensiveness fade away.

Luckily for me, the conversation moved on, as Jay wanted to know where the lunch had come from. Good cafes were worth sharing and if one place got a recommendation, they would often find most of the local police force descending on them for a taste. The Clock Square Café were in for a surge in customers now.

We worked away into the afternoon, as some dark-grey storm clouds started to loom on the horizon, casting shadows into the office. By 4 p.m., I had to put the lights on just to see; a drizzle of rain started to patter against the window. Since I was on my feet, I offered up another round of coffee to the guys and as they gave hearty yesses, my desk phone rang.

The front desk officer informed me I had a visitor downstairs. They had been put into Interview Room 2.

"Ooh," I said excitedly as I put the phone down. "Looks like my inquiries have paid off."

"I'll come," Jay offered, as he stood up and stretched.

"We'll all go," said Chris, rising to his feet too.

I scowled at them both.

"I can see to the visitor," I said. "If it's something important or whatever, I'll get you right away."

"Nice try." Chris held open the office door to me. "You can make the coffees and I'll deal with the visitor."

Downstairs, I discarded our three mugs in the break room and flicked on the kettle, before hurriedly rushing to the interview room, where Jay and Chris were just entering. Even as the door opened, I heard a woman's screech float from inside.

"Not them! I want that female detective! She's the one harassing my son!"

I immediately recognised Helena Brandon's voice. Knowing she meant me, I dutifully followed after Chris and Jay to face the music too.

Inside the interview room, not quite big enough for all of us, three people met Jay, Chris and me. Helena Brandon was already sitting at the table, with a face like thunder, and her husband, John, stood behind her, his hands resting on his wife's shoulders. Next to them, with a piecing gaze and sharp blue suit, was Melanie Georgiou.

"Detectives," she greeted us and shook hands with Chris and Jay stiffly as they took the two seats opposite. She gave me a pointed look, not extending her hand in greeting, and I was left with nothing to do but loiter behind them.

"Miss Georgiou," Jay said to the solicitor, a slight unease in his voice. "What can we do for you and your clients today? Come to give another statement regarding Yvonne Garrington's death?"

"Unfortunately, no," Melanie Georgiou replied with clipped words as she continued to shoot glares at me. "And if you wish to question my clients any more with regards to Yvonne's death, you will need to book an appointment. No, we are here about Detective Constable McArthur's conduct."

I stiffened at her words and straightened myself up as I found everyone in the room looking at me. I opened my mouth, mostly to ask her what the hell she was on about, but Helena Brandon beat me to it.

"Don't play dumb," she said, her voice full of venom. "You know why we're here. I explicitly told you yesterday *not* to talk to our son without us present, and what did you do this morning? You tracked him down hanging out with his friends to question him again. Without our knowledge!"

Melanie Georgiou fixed an unimpressed look on her face. "You are experienced officers," she said to Chris and Jay, "so you know how inappropriate it is for DC McArthur to continue to harass my clients' son without parental approval to speak to him. We've considered a formal complaint but at this time, I think a polite informal chat between us is all that's required."

"I didn't harass anyone," I cut in. That earned a glare from Chris and Jay, who were probably about to take a more diplomatic approach. "What? I didn't. I was looking for one of Jacob's friends when I came across him. We didn't even talk about the investigation. I simply asked if he knew where I could find his friend."

"That is questioning," said Georgiou. "Mrs Brandon had already made it explicitly clear to you that you weren't to do it without her present."

"It wasn't questioning."

"Anna," Chris growled at me. I wasn't helping.

"Was it pertaining to your current investigation?" Georgiou asked me. She knew the answer, and a thin smile crept across her face. "Of course, it was," she continued. "And as such, your conversation with Jacob Brandon could be considered illegal questioning of a minor."

"I didn't question Jacob!"

"Anna, stop!" Jay threw me a glare. He turned back to the Brandons, catching Chris's eye briefly as they exchanged looks. After a pause, he took a deep breath and tented his fingers on the desk. "We're sorry for any distress our investigation has caused your family, Mrs Brandon. Just know that, like us, DC McArthur's only goal is to bring justice to the person who murdered Yvonne Garrington. However, we'll make sure that any future inquiries are brought directly to you from now on."

For the first time since entering the room, John Brandon looked up at us detectives, and his gaze darted between us all. "But there shouldn't be any further inquiries, should there? You have the man who did it. I heard Yvonne's ex-husband broke into her house and killed himself."

Jay straightened up in his seat and Chris raised his eyebrows.

"Our investigation hasn't concluded yet," Chris said carefully.

"Well, why not?" demanded Helena. "He killed himself, he's clearly guilty. He was jealous of Yvonne's new lease of life and killed her. Once he knew you were onto him, he took action."

Chris gritted his teeth. "Our investigation is ongoing."

"Now now," said Georgiou as she looked at the Brandons. "Helena, John, despite the conduct of their constable, I am sure these gentlemen are competent detectives. These things rarely happen that quickly." With an infuriating clearing of her throat, the solicitor rose to her feet. She held out a card for Chris to take. "I'm sure you already have my number, but next time you need to ask my clients something, make sure you call me first. And I would appreciate it if only the most senior of officers dealt with them."

She gave another pointed look at me.

I pursed my lips together, unsure that I could control myself if any more jibes were thrown my way.

Following the solicitor's lead, the Brandons both stood straight and followed her to the door. Chris and Jay remained seated as they filed out. However, Helena paused as she passed Chris and leant in close to him, shooting a devilish look my way.

"Keep your dog on a better leash next time, Inspector."

\* \* \*

My mum and dad lived about half a mile from me, on a development of modern, crammed-in houses affectionately nicknamed the Herb Estate. The drizzly rain continued into the evening as I passed Rosemary Way and Fennel Crescent, and I found Dad in the garage, tinkering under the bonnet of Mum's car.

"Hey, sweetie," he greeted me as I parked up my old banger next to the open garage door and headed over. He threw one arm around my shoulder, avoiding touching me with his filthy, greasy hands, and kissed the top of my head. "Rough day at work?"

"How could you tell?" I asked.

Dad sniggered to himself. "You only turn up unannounced when it's been a bad day. Your mum is inside, dinner is almost ready. Got any plans for tomorrow?"

"Work," I groaned.

As punishment for embarrassing the team and earning a telling-off from the Brandons, Chris had left me a ton of tasks to do, including the most monotonous things he could scrape from the bottom of the barrel, such as tagging all the evidence on the online database and writing a hundred reports to go with it.

Inside their house, I found my mum in the kitchen, plating up three portions of chicken casserole. A glance at the dining table told me it was already set for three as well. She knew I would be coming somehow.

With barely a glance my way, Mum started chatting. "Hello, sweetie. Must have been a long week, I've barely heard from you. Did I tell you we're going to see a show in Norwich next week? We're going with Marie and Jack, and we'll have a nice meal beforehand. So, if you need me on Wednesday, I won't be at home. Not that you'll need me, you're a grown woman now, but you never know."

Mum turned from the worktop and faced me. Her cheerful grin didn't falter, even as she surveyed my grumpy expression. "There's wine in the fridge," she said, wiping her hands on the apron.

I didn't need telling twice and set about rustling in the drawers for the corkscrew. "How did you know I was coming?"

Mum gave me a knowing smile. "I'm your mum, I can sense these things. What's wrong?"

"I'm surprised you don't already know," I grumbled back. I was cautious not to give too much away.

Mum narrowed her gaze at me, hoping her intensity might make me crumble. "I didn't expect to see you today, I thought you'd be with the new boyfriend instead. You know, he's welcome to come to Sunday lunch tomorrow."

As an only child, I was more than used to my parents being keen to stick their noses into my business. Mum had figured out very quickly that I was seeing someone, although I had managed to keep the exact details from her somehow. She'd noticed the change in my demeanour, the shift in mood. As much as she pestered me to give her some details, I could tell she was also pleased that I was finding happiness again.

"Nice try," I told her. "I'm not inflicting you on him yet."

I hadn't spoken to Aaron all day and I wondered if he'd heard about the busy day and the telling-off. I was certain Chris would've told him. In fact, he would have probably heard Chris's bad mood from his own office, as the grumpy detective inspector made it very clear to me that I was 'not to go off against orders again'.

Mum pouted. "Oh, Anna! When are you going to introduce us? You can't hide him from us forever."

"I will when I'm ready, Mum." Or rather, when *he* was ready. Which wasn't looking likely to be anytime soon.

"You haven't even told us anything about him! Is he in the job, like you?"

"Yes."

"At the same station?"

"Mum," I cut her off. "I told you, it's early days."

"It's not though, is it?" Her eyes gleamed. "It's been a few months."

I narrowed my gaze at her. I knew that look; it was the same look she got when she was yakking away with her friends. Maybe she had set her gossip cartel out on a hunt for information.

"How do you know? Or rather, *what* do you know?"

"Nothing, nothing," Mum said hastily. "Just that it's been a few months. And he's in the police. That's all I know, I swear."

The front door closed and Dad entered the room, holding his greasy hands up like he was surrendering, being careful not to touch a thing. "Come on, sweetie, you know your mum. She has a way of finding out these things; her friends can crack any secret. No one is safe in this town."

Mum nodded along, as if I didn't know that already. "Yeah. You know, we found out recently that Charlie is moving to Wymondham. Marie had begged him not to take a job over there; she liked having him back home, but he took it anyway. Now it turns out that Sally's brother's wife works at the same place. She let the cat out of the bag to Sally."

"That's fascinating… Well, you have my blessing to use your friends to find out as much about my love life as you can." I gave Mum a smile, letting my confidence in her gossip crew's abilities hamper her knowing grin. "I'm pretty good at hiding things."

My secret had been safe for three months already. I was sure I could keep it safe from Mum and her gossiping book club for a bit longer.

"Ah, yes, but around here, everyone knows everyone. You can't hide something for long. We might not know who he is, Anna, but someone out there does. A neighbour, a friend. And I'll find out."

She had a good point. Although not a small area, West Norfolk was remote and insular enough for this to be true; it wouldn't be hard for her to find the truth if she really set her mind to it. Likewise, it wouldn't be impossible for her to find out about Sam's parole hearing if she really wanted to; that too was something I didn't want to deal with her knowing.

My parents had never liked Sam much from the beginning, but being a teenager at the time, I thought I knew best, and ignored their concerns. When Sam was arrested, my parents' first action was to put the house on the market and move us all away from the area. I didn't talk with them much after that about all that had transpired; it was a combination of bruised pride and their inclination to want to point out to me that they were right. We just sort of silently settled into an awkward state of not mentioning it ever again.

"Speaking of everyone knowing everyone," I said, keen to change the subject, "what do you know of the group who run the church and community centre on Nelson Avenue?"

"St Mary's?" Mum asked with a glance at Dad. He shrugged, indicating he had no idea. "I don't know much. I know John Brandon has something to do with them."

"Who's he?" asked Dad as he started to wash his hands in the sink.

"Oh, you know him. He's the one who owns that building firm, built all those new houses along Grimshoe Road last year. Anyway, Marie reckons that he's also got something to do with the fifty houses planned on the edge of town, on the old airfield site. The land belonged to the Cates family; they've farmed it for years. But Marie says a few months ago, John Brandon bought it for a fraction of what another developer had offered old man Cates for it and immediately put in a planning application for a new estate."

"You mean George Cates?" I must have looked more intrigued than I intended, as Mum nodded with a new gleam in her eye.

"That's right. He hasn't got any children, there's no more Cateses to do the farming once he's gone. Anyway, the planning committee are voting on it next week. Marie is in uproar about it."

"What's it got to do with her?" Dad asked.

"She doesn't like the idea of all the new traffic it'll bring through our estate. It'll make our road busier, she says."

"But we live down a cul-de-sac," said Dad.

"Oh dear," I said, but my conviction was lacking. "What about John Brandon's wife? Do you know her?"

Mum hummed thoughtfully. "Helena? Oh, yes, I've ran into her a few times. Marie calls her a nasty bitch."

Dad spluttered with surprise. "That's a bit strong for Marie."

"Yes, well, Marie and her both used to be on the parent fundraising group when the children were at school. Marie's youngest is the same age as Helena's boy. They clashed many times, and I can see why, Helena Brandon gives in to no one. She must be in control, no matter what."

"Do you think she's like that at the church group as well?" I asked.

"Oh, I'm sure of it." Mum pulled her face into a tight grimace. "Word is that Helena Brandon runs that place. Not the vicar, nor anyone else. There's nothing that goes on there that she doesn't know about. Did you hear about the vigil?"

"The what?" I frowned.

"The vigil. The church is holding a vigil at sunset for the lady who died recently, the one who was part of their church. I think it's tomorrow night. Anyway, it's causing a bit of a ruckus, because Helena is insisting only churchgoers can attend. There are plenty of neighbours and well-wishers who wanted to join in but have been told they can't."

"Not very Christian-like."

Mum bit her lip and shook her head. "Too right. I don't know what Helena Brandon thinks, but attending church every week isn't going to be enough to get her into heaven."

## Chapter Thirteen

I'd seen far more Sunday mornings at the police station than I would have liked, and just to add to the injustice, the weather was having a fair crack at pretending it was still summer. The sun was out, blazing hot, and a light breeze whipped clouds across the sky in trails of swirling white. The only saving grace for the day was the fact that I was alone.

No Chris, no Jay and no Maddie. I usually disliked working alone for so long, but today I was grateful to be left to my own devices. I could get over the embarrassment left from the Brandons the day before, plough through some work and not be checked up on by anyone.

I made it to almost lunchtime before I heard footsteps heading up the stairs to the office. I prayed for Aaron, the only person I was willing to put up with today, but I was disappointed when Chris entered.

"Oh... you're actually here." For some reason he said this with surprise.

"What does that mean?" I asked. I had a good stack of paperwork piled on my desk, showing just how productive I'd been. Every piece of evidence relating to our case was now thoroughly logged and cross-referenced. All except the things we were still missing lab reports for, such as the glasses and broken mug. We were still waiting to hear if any fingerprints or DNA had been recovered from them.

Chris shrugged as he pulled off his jacket. "I expected you would have gone off-task by now. You usually do. You're not great at focusing on orders."

"Yeah well," I said, feeling heat rise up my neck. "I'm working on my flaws." However, from the relaxed scowl on Chris's face, I could tell he wasn't really mad at me much now. Until the next time I pissed him off, anyway.

The shrill ring of my desk phone saved me from having to make small talk. I picked it up, feeling my heart rate rise with the prospect of something else to do. Another case? Another scene to investigate or crime to solve? Any distraction from having to talk to Chris was welcome.

"Visitor," the voice down the line said to me when I answered the phone. "Only wants to speak to you."

"Who is it?"

That garnered my co-worker's attention. Chris looked up from his computer.

"Brady Boston."

"Thank God."

At least it wasn't Melanie Georgiou or the Brandons again. I wasn't sure I could hold my tongue if it was them. I set down the receiver and Chris stared at me as I paused at the office door, each of us waiting to see who would give in first and break our uncomfortable silence.

Chris spoke. "Where are you going?"

"Brady Boston is downstairs, wants to talk to me."

"I'll come."

"I can do it myself–" I started, but a cutting look from Chris stopped me. It served as a reminder that he was my senior and after what happened with the Brandons, I couldn't be trusted. Great.

Dampening the grumble in my throat, I headed downstairs with Chris trudging along behind. I found Bos pacing the station foyer, shooting looks at the desk officer with a mixture of disdain and persecution. He didn't relent as I greeted him and showed him into an interview room. Today he wore a thick winter coat and mud-caked trainers.

Chris sat down next to me, and Bos gave him a distrustful glance. "I only want to talk to you," he said to me.

I shook my head. "Sorry, we come in twos."

To my relief, Chris kept quiet. He didn't seem keen to participate, which meant I could ask all the questions. Spending years building up a rapport, however feeble, with people like Bos rarely had pay-offs like this, and I was loath to share it. The more I looked at the young man, the more I noticed the strains of being homeless on him – the creases in his clothes, the dirt on his chin. I felt a pang of guilt. He may have been a nuisance when he was younger, but no one deserved to be thrown out onto the streets before reaching adulthood.

"So, you got my message that I wanted to talk to you?" I asked.

Bos shifted his suspicious gaze to me. "Yeah. You were one of the good ones," he muttered under his breath. "A pain in the arse, but you were always fair. Never tried to provoke me."

The young lad dropped his gaze to his lap, his eyes darting back and forth as though he was debating with himself.

"Bos, I know it's taken a lot of courage for you to come here, but you wouldn't have come to the station unless you needed to," I said.

"I'm no squealer," he said half-heartedly.

"Don't think of it as snitching to the police," I replied with a reassuring grin. "Think of it as helping someone who can't help themselves right now. What can you tell us about the death of Yvonne Garrington?"

Bos gave a heavy sigh, revealing just how downtrodden he was. For someone only days away from turning eighteen, he looked like the weight of the world hung on his shoulders. He was far too haggard, far too depressed for someone his age. Gone were his usual cheeky grin and the glint in his eyes. His brain wasn't working away to get himself out of trouble. He'd simply given up.

"I saw something, that night. The night that woman was killed. Someone went into the church." He slouched down in his seat until I could barely see him inside his worn, oversized coat.

"When?"

"Saturday night, probably early morning. Must have been about 4 a.m."

"Who?"

"I don't know."

"How do you know this?" Chris asked, his stern voice sending a shiver down Bos's spine.

I shot him a look and found he was now sat upright with intrigue. It was hard enough for the young lad to drag himself into a police station, let alone admit that he was homeless at the moment. This was a solid lead, and we didn't need to rub salt into his wounds by making him say it aloud.

Bos stiffened up as he clamped his mouth shut and glared at Chris. His hands twitched as he came very close to the edge, close to telling us where to go and storming off out of the room.

"It's okay, Bos," I said hastily. "We know. We know you've been sleeping behind the community centre, that your mum kicked you out. What we mean is, how sure are you that this happened? At 4 a.m., you say?"

"Of course I'm bloody sure," Bos snapped back but after a moment, his demeanour relaxed a fraction. "You ever slept on the streets? It's not an easy night's sleep. I hear everything."

"How many people?" Chris asked, still going for the blunt approach.

"I don't know. Definitely two. Could have been three. I only heard them talking."

"You didn't go and take a closer look?" I asked.

Bos shook his head stiffly. "You met those churchy bastards? Weirdos, the lot of them."

Neither Chris nor I had a comeback for that, so we just stayed quiet, probably both thinking the same thing; weirdos was an apt description. For a religious group, they never appeared very pious to me. They had a homeless person staying on their doorstep and either they hadn't noticed, or they didn't care.

"How long have you been sleeping rough?" Chris asked.

"A few weeks now. Maybe a month."

"That long?"

"Well, maybe it's been two months. It's been okay so far, it was summer. Nights are starting to get a bit cold, though. I even asked Jacob to ask his parents if I could sleep in the church at night – they have a key – but they said no."

"Have you ever heard anyone entering the church building at that time before?" I asked.

Bos shook his head. "No. Never. You can't get in anyway. It's locked."

"Who else has the keys?"

He shrugged, growing antsy at the barrage of questions. "Dunno. Not me."

"Bos," I said, placing my open palms on the tabletop. "Are you sure you didn't recognise the voices of the people you heard entering the church? What were they saying?"

But he shrugged once again, rolling his eyes over me as he wondered what exactly he was getting from this chat. Something had driven him here to help me, but whatever goodwill he had was rapidly disappearing. "I don't know, it was too muffled. I heard the door go, them talking. Twenty minutes later, they left, went by car. I didn't hear them arrive; I only woke up when I heard the door open. It creaks, like something out of a horror movie." He shivered and threw a half-hearted grin my way. "Can I go now? That's all I know, I swear."

I looked at Chris, who gave a curt nod, before rising to his feet. "You can go, Bos. Just leave your contact details here with DC McArthur."

Chris ended the interview and left the room, propping open the door as he went to make it clear to me that this was over. We'd gotten all the useful information out of Bos we were going to get, rather willingly on his behalf. I knew that wasn't easy for him to do, given his turbulent history with the police. Chris hadn't noticed how the young lad sank down further in his seat at the dismissal.

After a few minutes, when I was sure Chris was out of earshot, I asked Bos, "How did you get here?"

"Walked." He rolled his shoulders, as if it was no big deal.

"All the way to King's Lynn? That's over ten miles."

Bos smiled. "It's easy if you follow the river. Takes you straight here." He gestured behind him, where outside, the large, muddy River Great Ouse stood behind the station, beelining its way past King's Lynn town and out to sea. I supposed Bos was right, from Downham Market to King's Lynn it was a straight line to follow; plenty of walking paths along the riverbank. The landscape was a bit exposed but it was a lovely walk on a mild day like today.

"Do you want a lift home?"

Bos shook his head furiously. "I've had enough of cop cars."

But really, the unspoken part of his sentence stuck out the most; he had no home.

"Bos," I asked carefully, "have you ever heard of the night shelter?"

He nodded. "Yeah, in Lynn. For the homeless. I thought of that, they won't take me as I'm under eighteen. I'm social services' problem until then."

I could hear the venom in his voice. He hated social services; this was a kid who had had his fair share of dealings with them. Even when he was younger, I remembered he would disappear for a few weeks, then reappear. Whatever corner of the county social services had tried to ship him off to for a foster placement hadn't worked, and he always found his way back. Maybe now was the time to give him another chance at a much-needed fresh start.

I dropped my voice low. "I know the manager; I've worked on a few cases involving people who stay at the night shelter. They're a good bunch who work there. I'm sure they'd be willing to overlook a few days of not being eighteen as long as you keep your head down."

Bos bristled at my words and his face contorted with suspicion as though I'd just offered him a winning lottery ticket. "And what about you? You can't do something like that. You have to report me in as a homeless minor."

"True." I nodded. "And I will… tomorrow. Then, by the time social services get round to your case, you'll be eighteen and can tell them where to go. Plus, it'll take them longer to trace you if they think you're still staying behind St Mary's Church when you're really at the shelter."

The young lad eyed me cautiously, looking me up and down in an attempt to figure out the catch. But there was no catch. I just couldn't bear to see Bos spend another night under the stars. His childhood had been a mess until now; he could at least see in adulthood with the chance of things going better.

"You'd do that?"

I gave him a thin smile. "You helped me out with my case. I'll help you get a roof over your head. Come on, if you're quick, I'll buy you a coffee on the way."

"And some fags?" he asked hopefully.

"Don't push your luck."

\* \* \*

After making sure that Bos was suitably settled at the night shelter, I headed back to the station, where I found Chris had already called Jay and the pair were ready to head straight to the church.

"There are four sets of keys," Jay explained as he drove us there. I was relegated to the back as Chris took the passenger's seat. "Three are held by the church council;

Reverend Harding, the Brandons and George Cates, and the last set was held by Yvonne, as the cleaner. Hers are in evidence."

"Which set are we using?" I asked. I found it hard to believe Jay and Chris had managed to convince either of the Brandons to let us in.

"Reverend Harding will let us in. He's agreed to meet us there. He says he isn't aware of anyone entering the church building at that time of night."

"That doesn't mean he doesn't know anything. I really think we need to look closer into this church council," I said. "Yvonne was with them right before she died and spent most of her time with the group at the community centre, yet they all say they have no idea who killed her. And I've heard some rumours of an odd business deal going on between John Brandon and George Cates."

"What deal?" Jay kept his gaze on the road, but I heard the confusion in his voice.

"That Cates has sold some of his land to John Brandon for development at a much lower price than it's worth. Maybe they like helping each other out given they're all part of the same church."

I expected to be told to not speculate but to my surprise, Chris raised his eyebrows. "Interesting. We'll see what we find at the church and then go from there. When we get there, I'll talk to Reverend Harding and you two can take a look around."

We pulled up outside the church to find the community centre quiet and Reverend Harding waiting outside, key in hand. He greeted us all as we approached, his eyes lingering on me, before handing the ancient, long brass key over to Jay. Chris ushered the man over for a chat as Jay and I set to work.

Inside, the church was musty, with dust particles floating visibly in the air as the sun streamed through the stained-glass window at the far end by the altar. I wasn't an expert in churches, but the modernisation of this one struck me; it had comfy cushions and modern radiators interspersed along the aisle. It wasn't large, only two sets of pews either side of the aisle, with plush red carpet running up to the altar and pulpit. On the surface, everything looked immaculate, despite the age of the building and the dust I was sure plagued every surface.

Jay and I split up, him opting for the back of the church whilst I took the front. Once inside, we could hear nothing from the outside, not even the wind rustling the leaves of the two oak trees visible through the windows. Only my echoing footsteps pierced the silence, feeling wrong and out of place. I felt rude for the disturbance. Jay tried his best to be quiet.

The more I looked, the more the age of the church peaked through the modern additions. Underneath the carpet, tombstones and memorials poked out, in need of a polish. Cobwebs haunted the upper creases of the walls, where they met the arched ceiling, far out of reach. Several of the windows were cracked and patched.

Behind me, I heard Jay rustle and I turned to see what had caused him to make a noise.

"How often do you think they use this church?" he asked me, his voice floating down the aisle in the still air. I could just see him, nestled in amongst a bunch of heavy, thick red curtains at the back of the church.

"Every Sunday for morning service," I answered. I'd already checked the church and community centre timetables, committing them to memory when our investigation began. "Then the occasional wedding or funeral. Maybe a baptism. There's a much bigger church in town, St Edmund's, on the hill by the traffic lights. That gets used much more than this one."

"It's been mild lately, hasn't it? No need to turn the heating on yet."

"Huh?"

When my expression of confusion didn't get a reply, I headed over to Jay, where I found him leaning over the wrought-iron guard of an old stone fireplace hidden away in the recesses at the back of the church. He'd taken a pen out of his pocket and was poking the ashes, the smell wafting through the air.

"I can't imagine they use that old thing for heat," I said to him. "They have radiators. There must be a boiler somewhere too. Much more efficient."

"Then why has someone lit this fire recently?" he said. "You got any gloves?"

I handed him the pair I kept in my jacket pocket and with much less caution, Jay sifted through the fire pit.

He made a sound as something emerged from the ashes, a charred and discoloured object too large to be just a clump of charcoaled firewood. As he picked it up between his forefinger and thumb, I realised it was a piece of material. He unfolded it. It was – or rather, used to be – a piece of denim, still blue on the inside apart from an unnatural darker patch.

"I'm no expert," he said, "but I'm quite sure that dark bit is blood."

## Chapter Fourteen

My knowledge of forensic science only extended as far as how to properly handle evidence without contamination, so I had no idea if the dark patch on the denim material was blood, or whether DNA could even be recovered from it. However, when the scene-of-crime officers started arriving at the church, ushering me and Jay out of their way so they could get to work, they appeared very excited, so I guessed our development was a good one. They scoured the rest of the church, finding a few more pieces of fabric in amongst the ashes. As we regrouped outside,

Chris and Jay actually looked optimistic. In fact, this was the most optimistic I had seen them in days.

"Looks like we do need to look closer into the church group after all," I said as we stood in the churchyard, watching the proceedings.

Just outside of the gate, a crowd had amassed, mostly centred around Reverend Harding, who was desperately trying to tell people not to panic, and that the church was a sacred place, it was likely all a misunderstanding.

"Don't gloat," Chris snapped back, "it's not a good look."

He was just pissed that I was right.

As we observed the crowd, all with similar expressions of worry and shock, a sleek black Range Rover arrived at the community centre, taking up the disabled space right by the door. Out stepped John Brandon from the driver's seat, followed seconds later by his wife, who rounded the vehicle and stormed towards the churchyard gates.

"Let me through!" she demanded from the officer manning the line. "This is my church, I'm a council member and I can't believe you would do something so disrespectful and discourteous, on the Lord's day of rest, no less!"

"Now, Helena." Reverend Harding attempted to calm her down, but he very quickly stopped and slunk away to the back of the crowd. Even he wasn't willing to face her temper.

"This is outrageous. This is a house of God!"

From our congregation just a few feet away, Jay nudged me on the shoulder. "I'll cover your weekends for a month if you deal with her."

"No way," I said, turning my gaze to Chris. "I think this is one for the most senior officer on the team."

"Nah," he said back instantly. "United front. We'll all face the dragon."

Following his lead, and his cajoling, Chris, Jay and I made our way over to the churchyard gate, where the crime-scene cordon was in danger of being breached.

"Mrs Brandon," I greeted the furious woman with my best, self-satisfied grin. "May I ask what the problem is?"

John appeared at her shoulder, his expression matching his wife's but his mouth clamped tightly shut. Helena looked dressed for church, with a smart peach dress and tidy blazer jacket over the top. John wore a designer shirt and wayfarer glasses on top of his head. I noticed the crowd had taken a step back, allowing them a dignified space.

"You!" Helena turned her fury on to me, jabbing a finger over the line of crime-scene tape. "What is going on in there? You can't take over the church like this."

"Of course we can," Chris replied. "It's a crime scene. It contains evidence."

"But it's a house of worship! People need to be allowed in there to express their faith. And in times like this, to grieve and seek comfort in the Lord." She was really laying on the piousness today. She hadn't said anything so religious in any of our previous conversations.

Chris stood firm like a wall, folding his arms across his chest. "You'll just have to express your faith elsewhere for now."

"Well, for how long?" she demanded. "We have events planned. We have a vigil tonight! We were meeting at the church and marching through town with candles to show our solidarity, and our love for Yvonne. And to show our disapproval at such a horrific crime and your *inability* to bring the perpetrator to justice."

"The investigation is ongoing," said Jay, mirroring Chris's pose. Together they made an impenetrable barrier, and whilst I tried to hold my end of the line, I wasn't quite as impenetrable as them.

Either Helena Brandon realised that, or she just wanted to wind me up some more, but she skirted to the side, facing me.

"You knew this. You've done this on purpose, to prevent us from holding a peaceful protest." She gritted her teeth, almost snarling at me like Bruce the dog had done several days before. "I'll have you for this. All of you. This is religious persecution."

"Dear God, give it a rest," I said with a roll of my eyes. But that was definitely the wrong thing to say as Helena's face turned an impossible shade of purple.

"Blasphemy! Do not use the Lord's name in vain."

"That's it, get her out of here," Chris said.

The officer manning the line leapt forwards, more than happy to usher Helena Brandon away. Like a dog on a lead, John followed her, toeing the line carefully. The Brandons waltzed away and headed into the middle of the crowd, where they proceeded to rally some troops and began a playground-like game of glaring and whispering.

Chris let out an exhausted sigh, not relaxing his posture one bit. "What a nightmare that woman is."

Jay nodded in agreement. "We certainly don't need any accusations like that hampering us."

"She's hiding something," I said.

They looked at me with curious glances.

"There's a difference between hiding something and just being a dick to the police at any opportunity," Chris replied. "But still, one of us better go to this vigil tonight and keep an eye on things."

And quite predictably, they both smirked at me.

\* \* \*

"When you said let's go out tonight, this wasn't exactly what I had in mind," Aaron said, stamping his feet to keep warm.

The evening had turned chilly, and a bright moon shone above the rooftops, framed by a host of stars. A full moon. That usually meant trouble in the policing world, bringing with it a busy night shift with more craziness than we could keep up with. It was true what they said about the full moon bringing about madness; the word lunacy came from somewhere after all.

I scanned over the crowd, pleased to see there were enough people around for us not to be spotted. Probably about a hundred people had turned out for the vigil-slash-police-protest and I'd done my best to blend into the crowd. Puffy coat, woolly hat and a face full of make-up would hopefully be enough to keep me undercover. Aaron was fine – none of the church group knew who he was.

"Sorry," I said. "Blame Chris and Jay. One of these days, you'll have to assign them a new DC to boss around and give all the naff jobs to."

"Eh," said Aaron, tilting his head to the side. "I'll put up with the naff jobs for you… for now."

He shot me a grin with an amused glint in his eyes. I think we were slowly starting to get over the little hiccup from earlier in the week. I wasn't going to mention keys or commitment ever again, and instead was just going to focus my attention on finding murderers.

"So, fill me in," Aaron said as he leaned in close to me. Even at the back, we were keen not to be overheard. "The last thing I heard from Chris was that the prime suspect had killed himself."

"Mmm, true," I replied, watching the crowd.

Gathered outside St Mary's Church, a handful of people were making their way through the crowd, handing out candles. At the front, on a makeshift stage, Reverend Harding was rugged up in a thick black coat and scarf, and still shivering. Helena Brandon stood next to him, gazing over the crowd as if she was royalty. I spied John and Jacob Brandon milling around next to the stage, standing like bodyguards protecting a dignitary.

"Chris and Jay were quite convinced Keith Garrington was to blame, but I wasn't sure. This church lot just seem shifty to me. Anyway, I got a tip-off that someone had entered the church on the night of the murder of Yvonne, so we investigated and found bloody clothing in the fireplace."

"That explains why the church is off-limits." Aaron nodded over the heads of the crowd in front, where a pair of uniformed officers were manning the crime-scene line still, even at this hour.

"We've got to wait for more of the lab results which, going on the current rate of getting reports, could be in the next six months, but in the meantime, I'm going to keep digging into this church group. There are odd things about them – their hostility, uncooperativeness, rumours of strange business dealings. Whatever they're hiding, I'll find it."

Reverend Harding's voice floated over the crowd, the words lost to the night, but from the rhythmic droning, I assumed he was saying a prayer. I caught the word 'Yvonne' several times and murmurs of agreement ran through the crowd, before the whole group muttered a collective 'amen'.

"So what's the plan?" Aaron asked when the silence of the prayer subsided and chatter resumed.

A little old lady sidled up to us, handing us each a thin white candle with a paper trim around the middle to stop the wax falling onto our hands. The person offered a light, but Aaron waved them away, digging out his own lighter from his pocket.

"We'll just follow the crowd," I replied. "Stick to the back and keep our eyes and ears open. And keep an eye out for anyone looking particularly upset. We believe Yvonne might have had someone she was seeing."

From the back, it was harder to hear exactly what was being said on the stage but Helena Brandon was now speaking, her nose already rippled in disgust, so I assumed it was nothing good. Like a starry sky emerging from the cloudy night, the candles flickered to life. Then Reverend Harding and Helena hopped down from the stage, and taking their own candles, led the way from the church and down Nelson Avenue.

Aaron lit my candle and then his own, and we followed the flow from our place at the back. Reverend Harding had announced at the start of the proceedings that the route would go through town, disrupting the one-way traffic on its path, and end at the town hall where flowers would be laid for Yvonne. I had no idea if the location was meant to be significant in any way, or if the town council were aware of the floral carpet they were about to receive, but as far as protests went, this was a tame one.

A hymn started up from the crowd as we walked. I didn't recognise the words or tune but Aaron was humming along beside me. He quickly stopped when he realised I was watching him.

"Sunday school," he mumbled. "When you sing a song every week of your childhood, it sticks with you."

"I didn't know you were religious."

"I'm not." He laughed. "If anything, having it jammed down my throat every weekend made me as atheist as they come."

I spied a few spritely figures join the crowd towards the front of the procession, weaving between the candle-holders with the nimbleness of youth. When they jumped up, craning for a look, I realised it was Jacob Brandon's friend Ben, along with a few other lads. They walked with Jacob, sniggering and pushing each other.

"Fuck the police!" one shouted over the hymn, followed by a "Whoop whoop!" by another.

"Charming lads," I muttered under my breath.

They fell unexpectedly quiet right away.

A parting in the sea of people revealed Helena Brandon had made her way towards them and they'd hastily dispersed. Her furious glare was on Jacob, who shrugged and groaned at the injustice of receiving his mother's fury.

It took around thirty minutes to reach the town hall. Once there, the crowd fanned out into a semi-circle, with

Helena and Reverend Harding at the centre. With the poise of someone who had done ceremonies such as this her whole life, Helena went first, taking a bouquet handed to her by her husband and laying it silently on the ground by the door to the building. Harding followed her, and one by one, the crowd placed an array of flowers and cards down on the ground, saying a silent prayer as they did.

Aaron and I hovered at the side, keen not to get dragged in. As the last few people laid their flowers, Helena stood in front of the crowd, taking a deep breath.

"Bless you all for joining us tonight as we pay our respects to our beloved Yvonne. It breaks our hearts that we weren't able to do this in our sacred church, and hurts our souls even more to know that her killer will now never face justice for his actions. She will be dearly missed by each and every one of us. Join us now as we bow our heads in a moment of silence for Yvonne."

But she didn't bow her head. Instead, her eyes darted over the crowd, finding mine as though laser-guided. Recognition flickered over her face, along with incandescent rage at my very presence. I quickly blew out my candle and shifted to the side until I was hidden from her view for a brief moment.

"Time to go," I whispered to Aaron. I definitely didn't need another screeching at by Helena Brandon today. Hidden from my sight, I hoped she was staying at the front rather than making her way over to me.

Aaron blew out his candle and we stepped inconspicuously back until we were released from the crowd. Now free, we hurried back towards the street, where we could blend in with the Sunday night pub-goers and those queueing for takeaways.

"Are we going back to yours?" Aaron asked, just as I realised too that we were heading in no particular direction.

I glanced behind us and was relieved to see no sign of any Brandon. The crowd was breaking formation as the vigil ended.

"No way," I said. "I don't want those loonies knowing where I live. We're going to yours."

## Chapter Fifteen

The following morning, a group of chirping starlings woke me up at sunrise, just like every morning I stayed at Aaron's. They lived in the ash tree at the bottom of the garden, but Aaron was clearly used to them as they didn't rouse him. I padded my way downstairs and made myself some coffee, slightly giddy from the fact that I was now familiar enough with him to do this in his home. Still not familiar enough to have my own clothes here though, and pulling Aaron's dressing gown around me, I sipped my coffee as I wandered around downstairs.

Aaron wasn't one for much decoration, but he had a few photo frames on the mantel in the living room. One was of a smiling young woman, with a blonde-haired toddler on her lap, faded enough to make me believe the photo was of Aaron as a baby. His mother, possibly? He rarely talked about his family and only recently had I pieced together enough to figure the other photos out.

The most recent photograph of the lot was of a well-dressed family. This was definitely his brother; Callum looked like a slightly older version of Aaron, right down to the stoic, schooled expression on his face as he refused to smile. He had his arm around a beautiful, dark-haired woman, about the same age, and between the two of them, a young girl, with a bright smile and braces on her oversized teeth. Given that he didn't speak much about his family, I'd concluded that the Burns family weren't close, but there must have been someone out there Aaron wanted to introduce me to.

From a place in the kitchen where I'd set it on charge, my mobile started ringing, the shrill noise almost in competition with the relentless birds. It was Jay, *again*. These early-morning wake-up calls were getting so frequent, I was tempted to block his number, but when I answered, Jay was short but excited.

"Get to the station. We've got something interesting to deal with."

"The blood from the church has been identified?" I asked hopefully. If it was a match to Yvonne's then we could narrow in on the church council, the only people who had keys to the building.

"Not yet," he said, "but this is just as good."

Because he was a git, Jay refused to elaborate until I arrived at the station, which took me the longest out of the three of us as I had to go home first and get some clean clothes. When I arrived, Chris and Jay were in the office, giddy with anticipation.

"Guess who got arrested for domestic disturbance last night?" Jay asked me, leaping up from his desk like he'd actually found buried treasure.

"Who?" I couldn't possibly guess. Domestic disturbances were common and, as proven by Yvonne and Keith Garrington's past, it was the same story across the country; partners have a loud argument and concerned neighbours call the police. It was a bread-and-butter call-out.

"Helena Brandon. Apparently, just as the officers responded and her teenage son answered the door, she threw something at her husband."

"No way."

Even Chris chuckled at my expression. I shouldn't have been so shocked really; I knew better than most that domestic disturbances happened in all walks of life – from the most affluent people to the poorest. Even to future police officers. Human nature never changed. One of my very first call-outs was to a million-pound mansion in a village outside of Lynn called Grimston, belonging to some local businessman who had slapped his girlfriend. I enjoyed locking that tosser up for the night.

The same energy as Jay's surged through me; we had Helena Brandon in custody. Granted, it was on different charges, but still, there wasn't a better time to ask her about the material in the church fireplace than now. Her DNA and fingerprints would also be on file. *Yes!*

"Who gets to interview her? Please let me. I'll cover everyone's shift next weekend if you let me." Begging was not a good look, but I was desperate for a stab at Helena Brandon.

"Steady on," Chris warned us both, adopting a tone we usually only heard when he was on the phone with his teenagers. "We're not interviewing her."

"What? Why not?" I demanded.

"Because Melanie Georgiou has just arrived. They'll stall for ages, have plenty of consultations and refuse to answer any questions about anything other than the disturbance last night. She's not an amateur."

My heart sank at what Chris said. He was right, and the reality stung that Helena Brandon was within my grasp but there was nothing I could do. I shared a look with Jay, our disappointment deflating us. But when we turned back to Chris, a grin tugged on the man's lips.

"No, I've got a better idea. Now's the perfect time to speak to the husband whilst the solicitor is tied up." He grabbed a case file from his desk and motioned to me and Jay. "Come on, you can come with me, Anna. Jay, you stay and see what you can find out about what caused Helena's rage last night. Let's get going. Helena Brandon won't be in custody forever."

Not needing to be told twice, Jay bounded out the door with me close behind, pausing to grab the address for John Brandon from my computer.

\* \* \*

The Brandon family lived in Downham Market, down a leafy road called Park Lane. Their property stuck out like a sore thumb among all the other unassuming, semi-detached bungalows on the street. It was a monster, converted and extended, and partially hidden behind a six-foot brick wall. All signs of nature were absent; there were no trees, shrubs, or even weeds. Two large wrought-iron gates blocked our access and a small round video camera followed us from above as we approached and Chris rang the doorbell. The gates swung open. Whoever was inside was happy to talk to us.

Inside the compound, the Brandons' house sprawled across the whole plot, every inch immaculate and sterile. This family oozed perfection, or at least the image of it. The front door opened as we approached, swinging back on its hinges without a sound, and the figure of John Brandon filled the doorway. I faltered a step as he surveyed us with his mouth tightly closed as though he was gritting his teeth together, but Chris ploughed forward. We reached him and John Brandon stepped aside, turning his head a fraction too late for us to miss the raw cut above his eyebrow. He waved his hand in a gesture for us to enter and Chris dipped his head and stepped inside.

We were directed to a pristine sitting room and I almost felt like a fraud for daring to sit on the stark white sofa. A covert gaze around the room showed me little personality in the place – no family photos or trinkets. The place was as immaculate as a show home; and as emotionless as one too.

Chris settled in next to me and wasted no time in cutting to the chase.

"Nasty cut you have there, Mr Brandon. An injury from last night?"

John Brandon gave us a scornful look as he tenderly touched the wound on his forehead. "I knew you'd be here about that. It was just a disagreement. I don't want to press charges."

Chris shook his head slightly. "I'm afraid it doesn't work like that. Your wife was witnessed committing a crime; your wish to press charges or not is irrelevant. However, we're here for a different reason. We'd like to know more about Yvonne Garrington."

"What about Yvonne?" John asked, his face flushing with confusion but the rest of his body turning defensive. I could see his mind whirling away, wondering if we were trying to trick him by not pursuing questions about the assault.

"You knew her well?"

"Fairly," he said. Without his wife there to rebuff our questions, John floundered a little as he thought of things to say. "She was a friendly person. Bubbly."

"That's how everyone describes her," I replied. "We're finding it hard to believe that someone as well-liked as Yvonne could have been killed so viciously."

John shuffled under our gazes. "Well. We all know it was that ex of hers."

Chris ignored John's words and launched into another question. "Are you close with the other members of the church community? Pop round each other's houses, make business dealings, that sort of close?"

"We're all close, everyone in our community," John said stiffly. "We help each other out. If you're referring to the purchase of Cates's farm, then that's just business. It's all legal and above board, our solicitors have made sure of that."

"Did Yvonne ever ask for someone to help *her* out?" I asked.

Chris glanced at me out the corner of his eye but made no other move, curious to see where I was heading. His question about how close the church community was had prompted a query of my own; how much exactly did they help each other out? When I considered my own colleagues, I realised we went quite far to help out one another. Chris helped Jay move house a year ago, Aaron rescued me when my car broke down. Those were normal, friendly interactions. Business dealings which cost the seller a significant amount of money weren't quite so normal.

"With what?"

"Money, a job. She was in financial dire straits after her husband left her," I said.

With a slight nod of his head, Chris caught my drift. "If you are willing to help each other out with business dealings, selling land to one another, then surely someone helped Yvonne out with her money problems?"

"I guess, when you put it like that…" John Brandon folded his arms across his chest, but it did little to hide his discomfort. "I gave Yvonne a job. She did a bit of bookkeeping for me."

"And how long had she done that for?" asked Chris, not missing a beat.

"A few months, maybe six. She was helping a lot with this purchase of Cates's land."

"Did Helena know this?"

"Everyone knew," John said. "Even Cates knew, he approved of it. In fact, he's such a crotchety old man, I think Yvonne was one of the reasons he agreed to it. He liked her."

"So, you spent a lot of time with Yvonne recently?"

"Not really… She didn't have a computer, so I used to bring my laptop round for her to use. Everything is electronic nowadays."

"Was that all that used to happen during your visits?" I asked.

John looked at me with an overwrought, confused frown.

"Pardon?"

"Did you only drop a laptop off? Or was there something more to your relationship with Yvonne?"

"No," he said instantly. He broke eye contact with me and turned to Chris, his round eyes imploring to be believed. "I swear, whatever you're thinking, that wasn't the case. It was only work. Nothing else."

Chris hummed; the noise too low for John Brandon to hear but enough for me to recognise what he was thinking. "Mr Brandon, we're going to need to see that laptop, along with any other communication you shared with Yvonne. Any texts or call logs, business-related or otherwise."

John nodded keenly. "Of course."

Chris didn't dwell on John's eagerness to help. However, from past experience, we couldn't even have a conversation with this family without their solicitor intervening. I doubted John would really hand over private correspondence without a search warrant compelling it. Unless John wasn't the obstructive one of the Brandon family; maybe it was Helena who had hired Melanie Georgiou to protect her family from the investigation.

"What was your argument about with your wife last night?" Chris asked, taking advantage of John's willingness to help.

"You said you weren't here about that."

"Unless it was about Yvonne." He sat up in his seat, leaning close to John Brandon as the man babbled for an answer. He was off guard, and Chris knew that, so he let an uncomfortable silence settle over us, creating pressure, until John finally answered.

"It wasn't about Yvonne," John said firmly, far more adamant on this than on anything else he'd said so far. "It was about Jacob. Helena wants to send him to boarding school."

"Why's that?" I asked. It was September; the new school year had just begun.

"She thinks the lads around here are bad influences. Sending him away might stamp out some of the bad behaviours Jacob has been displaying," said John as he wrung his hands together. "He's been smoking, skipping school, sneaking out at night."

"Sounds like a teenager to me." Chris snorted. "I would know, I have two teenage sons myself. You can't watch them every minute of every day. They're bound to find mischief."

"Yes, well," John continued, "it doesn't really fit with Helena's image. We're leaders in the community, I'm on the board of governors at the secondary school. We have standards. My point was that it wasn't a good enough reason to send him away."

"Helena must have quite a temper on her."

"Well, she's just… she wants what's best for our family."

"Does she often react violently?"

"Never." John shook his head fiercely. "Helena wouldn't hurt a soul."

"Except for you," I said, gesturing to his forehead.

John touched his wound again, still red and swollen, before his fingers darted away. "It was an accident," he said with a newfound assuredness. "Helena wouldn't hurt me. We love each other."

Chris bristled very slightly next to me. He reached inside his pocket for a contact card and jotted down his email address on the back, before handing it to John. He didn't appear convinced by John's answers, but then it was hard to tell exactly what he was thinking.

"Please, bring us that laptop as soon as possible," he said as he rose to his feet, and I followed him to the door.

Chris stopped at the doorway and turned back to John, who still sat with his arms crossed, reluctant to move. "Do you have a key for St Mary's Church?"

John nodded hollowly. "Of course. We keep it with our set for the community hall. Why?"

"No reason," Chris said quickly, surprising me as he turned for the door without another word.

Once free of the Brandon compound, the iron gates closing silently behind us, Chris slid into the driver's seat of his sensible family car. He wasn't too keen to make a move, though, and stared ahead at the street as a persistent breeze released the leaves from the trees, turning the road into a blanket of orange and brown.

"Why didn't you push John Brandon about the key to the church?" I asked.

"We already know they have a key, there was no point in questioning him further," Chris said, his gaze still ahead. "Both him and his wife are keen to uphold their image and reputation. The pillars of the local community, churchgoers, business owners. How far would they go to protect that image?"

"Enough to lie to us?" I offered. "Enough to kill?"

"Any of it seems possible."

"And what about Keith Garrington?"

Chris breathed deeply and turned the key in the ignition, the engine sparking to life. "The problem we have is that no one fits neatly as responsible for this crime. Keith had motive, kind of – regret, jealousy, financial incentive. The Brandons and the rest of the church group have means. But we're still lacking hard evidence. Until we can prove who was in Yvonne Garrington's house that night, or who entered the church to dispose of their bloody clothing, we're no closer to pinning this on anyone… yet."

I liked the way he said *yet*. Chris wasn't one for rousing speeches, but just that one small word showed me he hadn't given up. The mystery would slowly unfurl itself, we just had to help it along.

As we drove away, the display of the car lit up as a call came in from Jay. With the press of a button, his voice filled the cabin.

"I listened in on the interview of Helena Brandon," he said, launching straight to it, "and whilst I did that, I also ran a background check. Helena has two previous charges of public disorder on her record, from when she was in her early twenties."

"Let me guess," said Chris, "involved in either lewd or violent behaviour whilst out drinking. Nearly every charge of public disorder at that age is down to a boozy night."

"Pretty much," Jay replied. "She was sentenced to a community order and anger management sessions. Seems Helena Brandon has a temper on her."

"That was the impression I got from her husband too," I said, "no matter how much he tried to downplay it."

"That's not all," Jay continued, sounding like he was on the clock to get all the information out. "Helena Brandon was adamant that last night's argument was due to John working too much and not spending enough time with the family."

"Oh really? Well, he told us a different story, said it was down to Helena wanting to send Jacob to boarding school," I replied.

"So, at least one of them is lying about what caused their falling-out last night." Jay's voice turned gleeful. "What's the betting that it was neither of those things but something to do with the blood found in the church?"

"Any more results come back from the lab yet?" Chris asked.

"Not yet," said Jay.

Chris grumbled with disapproval under his breath. "How are things going with the domestic disturbance charge?"

"She's given a statement, just waiting for charge and bail now. Some genius out there has decided risk factors are low and there's no need to detain her any longer," replied Jay.

"Stop them," Chris said curtly. "Don't let them release her yet, not until we've spoken to her."

"And how am I meant to do that?" Jay scoffed down the line.

"I don't know. Tell the custody sergeant to drag his feet with the paperwork, ask for a re-evaluation of the risk factors. Just keep her there."

"Why?"

"I've got an idea," said Chris, and he put his foot down on the accelerator.

## Chapter Sixteen

Chris knocked urgently on Aaron's office door and forged inside at his beckoning. I followed, not sure what his idea was but very eager to find out. I rarely saw Chris so energised.

Aaron was at his desk, yawning at whatever paperwork he was reading and sipping from a steaming mug of tea. "Hi?"

He raised his eyebrows at us. We hadn't even stopped by the office to discard our jackets yet. Chris was a man on a mission.

"I need you to call the lab," Chris said, straight to the point. "Pull out the DCI card and get those blood results back ASAP."

Aaron looked at me and I shrugged back, just as bewildered as he was; then, he smirked with bemusement.

"You've got an idea?" he asked knowingly.

Chris nodded. "We can safely assume that the blood found in the church belonged to Yvonne, but with a dragon like Melanie Georgiou downstairs, we need solid proof in order to question Helena Brandon. She's got a criminal record and a key to the church. We need that lab confirmation before we speak to her. We need proof the church was used in the murder of Yvonne Garrington."

"And who's going to interview her?" Aaron asked.

"Oh, please let me," I said, bouncing on my heels. "Please, please, please."

Chris threw a look my way, almost like he had forgotten I was there. He looked between Aaron and me, internally weighing up something, before giving a considered hum.

"No," he decided. "You can make a round of coffee though. And then remind John Brandon about that laptop. Push him to send those correspondences with Yvonne before his solicitor finds out."

Crestfallen, I pouted back, about to argue and make my case, but Chris stopped me in my tracks with a sharp glare.

"Harsh," Aaron muttered under his breath, but he too received the sharp glare, and hastily picked the phone up and started to dial the number for the lab.

As I retreated from the room, I heard Chris grumble at Aaron, "You need to be less obvious."

"Huh?" Aaron's voice filled with confusion.

"That stupid smile on your face," said Chris as he headed out the door after me.

Thirty minutes and a strong coffee later, Aaron entered the Serious Crime office, throwing a paper file at Chris and being careful not to look at me.

"Not every team gets the DCI printing out their files for them," he said. "Just make sure this is enough to get her. If she killed Yvonne Garrington, I don't want her walking free out of this station."

"Yes, boss," said Chris and he scooped up the file with nothing else other than a determined look scrunching his face. "The blood was a match to our victim. No prizes for guessing that one. No other DNA recoverable. Come on, let's go."

\* \* \*

Relegated to the observation room once more, I settled in to watch Chris and Jay, keen to see how they would play this. If I hadn't known any different, I wouldn't have guessed Helena Brandon had spent most of the night in the police station. She looked as prim and proper as always, still well-dressed from the vigil the night before, and not a hair out of place. I might have felt jealous at her ability to look so composed, if it wasn't for the bitchy scowl plastered across her face.

Next to her, Melanie Georgiou looked just as put-together in an olive-green trouser suit. They really put me to shame in my standard black trousers, white shirt with the tiny coffee stain, and sensible ponytail. But then, I was behind the one-way mirror observing the interview room, so there was no way they could see me and judge me like I was judging them.

Before Chris and Jay could even sit down, Melanie Georgiou was on the attack.

"Any questions you ask must be in relation to my client's current charge," she said. "We're not here to answer anything about your murder case."

"Don't worry," said Chris, "we'll stick to asking about the domestic disturbance last night." And he looked to Jay, giving a small nod as if to start the race.

Jay cleared his throat. "So, tell us again, what was the argument with John about?"

"My husband. He's been working far too much lately."

"Is that so? Because your husband tells us it was about sending your son to boarding school."

"An argument can be about more than one thing," Helena snapped back, not missing a beat.

Her expression denoted her patience was wearing thin and the appearance of Chris and Jay threatened to tip her over the edge. From the way Melanie Georgiou sat poised, pen in her hand, she knew this too.

"But it must have been bad for your neighbours to call the police," said Jay.

"It was heated."

"That's understandable. Sending your son away to boarding school is a big decision."

"I would never do that," Helena said, resentment in her tone. "I love my son; I do everything for him. I drive him to school, I arrange his appointments, I organise his football team. John was wrong to even suggest it."

"Ah." Jay gave a wry smile, gone again in a flash. "See, the inconsistencies begin here. John told us it was *your* idea to send Jacob away. So, if you're lying about that, what was the argument really about?"

"My client isn't lying," spat Melanie Georgiou. "She has just misremembered a heated argument with her husband."

"Was the argument about Yvonne Garrington? You didn't tell us that your husband had hired Yvonne as his bookkeeper."

Chris rested his palm on the file containing the lab report on the table. He tapped it intermittently as Jay spoke, as if willing Helena Brandon or Melanie Georgiou to ask what was in it.

"Because she wasn't the bookkeeper, I am," Helena replied, her teeth gritted together. "I deal with all financials for the firm. John just wanted an extra bit of help for this deal with George Cates. It's almost finished, anyway. Yvonne had done her part; the paperwork is complete, and the land is ours. We're just waiting for the planning permission."

"Still," Jay continued, "John and Yvonne must have spent some time together whilst working on this deal. Did you argue about the amount of time they spent alone? You didn't think to tell us at any point that your husband had business with Yvonne outside of the church group?"

"It wasn't relevant." This time, Helena looked to her solicitor for confirmation. "As I said, the deal is done."

"When did John and Yvonne discuss their business relationship? At church? During the evenings? Did Yvonne come to your house to discuss or did your husband go to hers?"

Helena opened her mouth, almost fit to burst, but Georgiou cut in. "I don't like where you're going with this. Are you trying to insinuate that my client's husband was having an affair with Yvonne Garrington?"

Jay shrugged, a boyish grin tugging at the corner of his mouth as he glanced at Chris. "I didn't say that, but it could cause a hell of an argument, lots of emotions flying through the air – emotions and objects. And we do have good reason to believe Yvonne was having sexual relations with *someone* from the condoms we found in her house. We've seen it happen time over; colleagues working late at night, sharing the stresses and successes of the work. Family at home just don't understand. It's surprisingly common. There's no reason to hide it if that was the case."

"Not *my* husband," Helena declared. "We've been married nineteen years; we are happy together."

"You didn't seem happy together last night when you launched a wine glass at his head."

Melanie Georgiou cut in, hissing like a venomous snake. "My client hasn't confirmed the argument was about Yvonne Garrington last night."

"Your client hasn't denied it either."

"There was nothing going on between my husband and Yvonne. *Nothing.*" A small amount of spit flew from Helena's mouth and landed on the table. She caught herself at that moment, pulling back in her seat and shooting a stern look at her solicitor, as if to will her to make the two annoying detectives go away.

I sucked a coarse breath between my lips; this was the first sign that we were making headway. She was starting to crack.

Jay shared a look with Chris – this conversation was going exactly the way they wanted it to. Chris took the chance to finally speak.

"When was the last time you used your key to enter St Mary's Church?"

Thrown by his question, Helena glanced at her solicitor. "I don't know. Why?"

"That's not at all relevant," said Georgiou indignantly.

"It could be," said Chris.

"In what possible way?"

"Well, you do have a key, don't you?" Chris said to Helena.

She nodded, the movement so rigid I wondered if she had ever nodded before. She watched with wide eyes as Chris slowly removed the lab report from the file and slid it across the table. "We know you have a key – your husband already told us that. We have evidence that someone used the fireplace in the church to dispose of the bloody clothing they killed Yvonne in."

"Well, it wasn't me! I only have a key for emergencies, Reverend Harding usually unlocks and locks the church. You should be asking him."

"This is *not* relevant," Melanie Georgiou interjected, placing one hand on Helena's arm to settle her down.

Helena Brandon threw the hand off, throwing pointed glares at each person in the room, even her own solicitor.

"Reverend Harding doesn't have a history of violent outbursts. You do," Chris said. He ignored the solicitor and removed another paper from his case file, presenting it across the table. They scanned over the conviction list, detailing Helena Brandon's public disorder offences from two decades prior.

"That's history," Helena said, throwing the paper back before her solicitor got a good look.

Melanie Georgiou snatched the conviction list from Chris's grasp and turned to the woman next to her. "I think I need a moment alone with my client in light of these new disclosures."

Holding in a sigh, Jay and Chris suspended the interview and headed outside, leaving the two women to discuss the case in hand. I caught up with the guys in the corridor, heading to the break room.

"What did you notice?" Jay asked slyly, with a grin like a child told to keep a secret.

"She lied," I replied. "She said it was John's idea to send Jacob to boarding school, but John said it was her idea."

"Or maybe her husband lied, and she's telling the truth," said Chris over his shoulder as he forged his way to the kettle. "We don't know which one is lying yet. Could be that they both are."

"Helena's lying, definitely Helena," I said. "She's *this* close to losing her rag and admitting it."

Jay nodded in agreement.

"I don't think we're going to get her to admit to anything," said Chris, ever the pessimist. "She's hell-bent on protecting her image, she'll lie through her teeth. We already know she's got a temper on her. I'm liking her for it the most out of all the people who hold keys for the church. The only thing we can't pinpoint is a motive. Why kill Yvonne?"

"Jealousy?" I offered. It was an age-old motive for murder. "Maybe Helena Brandon grew jealous of the time her husband was spending with the victim."

"Or maybe it has something to do with this land deal," said Jay. "It sounds like George Cates was being screwed over by the Brandons, accepting an offer for the land that was considerably less than it's worth. Maybe Yvonne found out and stood up to Helena."

I nodded along with him. "I can't imagine that would have gone well."

"Then we'll ask her about it next," said Jay, his excitement growing.

Chris gave a measured hum as the kettle came to a boil. He waved a mug at Jay, who shook his head back, too eager to settle for a brew. Only after making himself a black coffee and taking a deep sip, did Chris reply.

"We won't be getting through Melanie Georgiou unless we have more info up our sleeves. She'll want to give a prepared statement and end the interview to stop the risk of Helena losing her temper and giving away something she shouldn't. Before we go back in, Jay, call George Cates and see what you can find out about this land deal from him. Exactly how much money did he miss out on by selling to the Brandons. And, Anna…"

He trailed off as he realised there wasn't much that he could give me to do. The obvious person to speak to was Jacob Brandon, the only other witness to the fight and the only one who would know what it was really about. But I wasn't allowed to speak to Jacob.

"Get lunch," said Chris, quickly turning his attention back to his steaming mug. "When you get back, we'll attempt round two with Helena and her solicitor. It won't hurt to let her stew a bit longer."

## Chapter Seventeen

*Get lunch.* Was that all I was good for now? Chris's words grated on me so badly that I decided I would get lunch; I would get it as far away as I possibly could, and drag my heels whilst doing it. I thought I was finally making headway in earning his trust but clearly, I was still only useful as a team skivvy.

Pettiness wasn't a good look for anyone, including me, so with a front seat loaded with sandwiches from the nice cafe that Jay liked, I decided to use my time out of the office wisely and stopped by St Mary's Church and community centre. Maybe I could dig out a little info about the Brandons and this land deal from the rest of the congregation.

Although the community centre was usually closed on Mondays, I found Reverend Harding outside, staring wistfully at the church as the crime-scene tape blew in the wind and leaves floated down from the oak trees into the churchyard. As I parked up and made my way over to him, I felt a pang of sympathy. He was a preacher without a pulpit. However, it was only temporary, and I was sure the church would be released as a crime scene soon enough.

Hopefully once someone finally copped to Yvonne's murder.

Reverend Harding shivered as I joined him, and gave a yearning, doleful look my way.

"Detective."

"Sorry about the church, Reverend," I said. The rest of the premises were peaceful, with the same ancient atmosphere that I felt inside the building.

"It's understandable," he replied, still with a hint of sadness. "It's alarming to me that such a place of kindness and respect could be desecrated in such a way. To be privy to a crime…"

"I have a feeling the murder isn't the only crime going on around here under your nose."

The reverend gave me a distressed stare, repulsed by my outright claim. I didn't mean to upset him, but I found it hard to believe he could be the leader of the flock and not have some inkling of what was going on around him. Either he knew and turned a blind eye, or he was involved.

"What can you tell me about this land deal between the Brandons and George Cates?"

Harding sighed, sagging under the weight of the world. He returned his gaze to the church building, eyes climbing up the steeple until the weak sun blinded him.

"Not a lot, I confess. I knew of it, but not the details. George is getting on; the farm is more of a burden than anything else nowadays. I feared that John and Helena may have taken advantage of that fact, but I dismissed those sullied thoughts. These are good people. They give so much back to the local community. I refuse to believe…"

His voice travelled off, lost to the wind. Cinnamon-coloured leaves fell around us, whirling past as though they were daring each other to see who could get closest. I waited for the reverend to pick up his train of thought again.

"I'm sorry," he said. "It's just been such a shock. To think that this has all happened and that someone close could be responsible… It's really shaken my faith."

I gave the reverend an empathetic smile. "*Do not murder, do not bear false witness*. Those are some of the basics, so I can understand why you feel that way."

"Maybe I didn't teach my flock well enough," he mused.

"Don't think like that," I replied. "You cannot take responsibility for another's actions."

He shivered as a gust of wind rustled the trees. Harding motioned to the community centre hall and I followed him, not bothered by the chill in the air but not wanting him to feel any more uncomfortable. He let us into the foyer and the cold was instantly shut out.

"Does your faith ever feel tested, Detective Constable?"

I pursed my lips, not sure how to respond. I didn't want to outrightly tell the reverend I wasn't much of a religious person, having never spent long wondering about a god, afterlife or anything else. But then I supposed his question was open-ended; maybe he meant my faith in what I did, rather than what I believed.

"Sometimes," I admitted, remembering with distaste the time – not too long ago – when I had no faith in myself or my abilities. I had pulled myself out of that slump, with a little help from my friends and family, and was now happier than ever. "I think it's only human to question ourselves."

"Yvonne had restored my faith to its fullest. When she joined us a year ago, she was a shadow of herself. She emerged as time went by and embraced life for what it was. She found happiness in her faith. Happiness in herself. There is nothing more glorious than watching people change for the better, however long it takes."

I mused on the reverend's words. Did everyone have the capacity to change? Maybe Keith Garrington had changed, had realised the error of his ways and was truly sorry for the way he'd treated Yvonne.

Maybe Sam had changed. Maybe I needed to give him a chance at this parole board hearing.

"Reverend," I said, "didn't you say that Yvonne helped out at the groups in the community centre?"

He nodded. "Yes."

"And that Yvonne wanted to set up her own group?"

He nodded again, a pensive look retaking his face. "Yes. She was quite set on the idea. She wanted to start a social group for people who had experienced trauma. A survivors' group, she called it."

A survivors' group. A place for her to meet and support other people who had gone through the same abuse she had.

Harding carried on. "She had only floated the idea though. Helena and a few others had nixed it, unfortunately, although they had a valid reason. They suggested the group needed to be run by a trained professional."

"And how did Yvonne take that?"

"Oh, it wasn't going to stop her." He gave a wistful smile. "She was determined to help people; she said she'd find another way to do that. Yvonne always said the world had two types of people – monsters and saviours. She wanted to be a saviour… and someone took that chance from her."

The world certainly had some monsters, I could agree with that. But it wasn't so black and white. No one person was bad or good, we were all a mixture of both, shaped by so many factors and influences.

Who did Yvonne think of as a monster?

"Sorry, Detective," Reverend Harding said, interrupting my thoughts. "I didn't mean to bring down the mood. As always, I'm happy to help with your inquiry but I have an appointment in half an hour with a young couple due to get married. Can we talk more afterwards?"

I gave the reverend my friendliest smile, and he relaxed, his troubles lifting a fraction.

"Of course. Shall we meet at the station? I'll have a nice cup of tea waiting."

"That would be very kind," he replied. "I look forward to seeing you then."

On the scale of monster to saviour, it was easy to see where the reverend sat. He, at least, was truly sorry Yvonne's life was cut short just as she settled on the road to positive change.

I was about to leave when something caught my eye. The colourful display on the wall of the photos from the choir concert still sang a tune of joy and camaraderie, every face smiling. Yvonne was absent from them all. The reverend watched me as I took each one in.

"Who puts up these photographs?" I asked.

"I believe Helena did," said Harding. "We always like to show off the fun times had here, entice more people to join."

One photo forced my gaze back to it. On the surface, it was innocuous. It was a group of people, either setting up or striking set, on the stage in the hall. I recognised it by the musty curtains. They'd struck a pose for the camera, but someone was caught in the corner of the frame, carrying a stack of chairs so high they almost obscured his face. Almost, but not quite enough to hide the thick-rimmed glasses he wore.

"Is this Jacob?" I asked the reverend, tapping on the photo.

Harding leaned in for a better look. "I believe so."

"Does he always wear glasses?"

"Oh no." Harding laughed to himself. "He's a typical teenager, thinks they make him look uncool. He only puts them on when his mother chastises him into doing so."

The glasses found in Yvonne's kitchen were Jacob's.

He had been there that night.

I prized the photo from the board, careful not to tear it. I bid Reverend Harding a hasty goodbye as the revelation struck me and I hurried from the community hall, desperate to share my findings with Chris and Jay. If we could prove the glasses belonged to Jacob, then that placed him at the murder scene. Was his mother covering for him? Who else was involved?

We had a small amount of time to get ahead whilst Helena Brandon and Melanie Georgiou worried about the other details of the case. But I knew from the deep palpitations in my chest that I was on to something good, and I had to get through to Chris and Jay before they went back into the interview room.

As I strode to my car, I pulled my phone out, calling Jay and willing him to pick up. It rang and rang. Damn it. Maybe they'd already gone back in.

Just as a computerised voice told me to leave a message after the tone, I felt a hand grip my shoulder from behind. I spun on my heels and came face to face with Jacob Brandon.

His expression matched his mother's – thinly concealed disgust and fury. No matter how hard he tried, it edged its way in. I stuffed the photo and my phone back into my pockets, as Jacob squared up to me, forcing me back a few steps. His teeth gritted together, making his jaw jut out just like his father. One fist was shaking by his side and the other slowly, conspicuously, drew out a shiny chrome kitchen knife from behind his back. It reflected my alarmed face back at me perfectly.

"Jacob," I said carefully.

I weighed up my options: I could run – my car was nearby – or I could fight, but that was a last resort. The best-case scenario was to convince him to come in peacefully, and I'd deal with the consequences of ignoring my orders and arresting him later.

However, these options didn't seem to play in Jacob's head like they did in mine.

"Jacob," I said again, a warning in my voice, but holding my hands up.

I'd learnt from experience that I was no match for a knife. My old injury tingled just with the thought of it. Whereas a slightly younger and naive Anna would have tried to disarm him, I knew my best option was to comply. Maybe I could convince him to come in once he'd calmed down.

Speaking through his deadlocked teeth, Jacob spun me round so my back was to him, and he pressed the knife into my lower back, under my jacket. "Come with me."

## Chapter Eighteen

It didn't take me long to realise that Jacob had no plan – he was sixteen years old, not a criminal mastermind. He marched me through one of the alleyways between the church and the cottages, the uncomfortable coldness of the knife pressing against my skin. Out of the alleyway and immediately left, Jacob steered me right to the building site where two houses were being constructed. Today the site was deserted, no workmen in sight. A sign was affixed to the scaffolding around the shell of the first house – *Brandon Building Services*.

Tarpaulin flapped in the wind as Jacob shoved me down a muddy path to the back of the first property. The back door was missing, revealing just dusty, plasterboard-covered walls inside and a few discarded building materials. With a jab, Jacob forced me through what I guessed would become a kitchen and upstairs to a nondescript room. The window was covered with a blue plastic sheet. Jacob gave me another robust shove.

Catching myself before I fell head over heels, I held my hands up in surrender. At least without the knife against my back, I could keep it in sight. Jacob didn't hold it like a pro, but it didn't take an expert to inflict some damage.

"Jacob," I said cautiously, hands high in the air. "Jacob, I know you're scared right now, but no one has to get hurt. Just put the knife down."

"You think I did it?" he asked, but his tone was more accusatory than surprised. "You think I killed Yvonne?"

"Those were your glasses we found in her kitchen, weren't they?"

"Damn it!" he spat, and started to pace relentlessly in front of the door. "Those fucking glasses."

"So, did you, Jacob?" I watched him go back and forth, faster and faster. "Did you kill Yvonne?"

He didn't slow down, pacing across the room. Still waving the knife in one hand – its metallic glint catching my eye as I tried to take in the surroundings and measure for an escape – Jacob pulled out his mobile phone. I couldn't see the screen when he held it to his ear, but whoever answered only gave a single-syllabled grunt.

"Get over to the site on Snape Lane," said Jacob, leaving no room in his voice for a refusal. "Now."

He shut off the phone and slipped it back into his hoody pocket.

"Who was that?" I asked. It could have been any one of his friends. Maybe I was wrong and Bos wasn't the gang leader after all; maybe it was really Jacob Brandon and Bos was just the frontman.

When Jacob didn't answer me, I tried again with the calming words. "Jacob, just put the knife down. We can talk about this. I don't know how your glasses got into Yvonne's kitchen but if something happened that night, I can help you."

"Help?" he cut in, spit flying. "How can you help, you're a copper. You don't help, you just persecute people."

Hmm, it seemed that Jacob had inherited his mother's distrust of police.

"You're underage, Jacob. There are things I can do, people I can get in touch with. You don't have to do this alone."

"I'm not alone," he spat, his fury making him froth at the mouth.

Not once did he stop pacing, only risking small glances my way, to check I hadn't moved too much from my position. I had few options where I was. The window was sealed and there was nothing but a muddy building site below. Jacob blocked the stairs. The only weapons at my disposal were a stack of plasterboard and an empty cement bucket.

And my mobile phone.

I reached inside my pocket, wrapping my fingers around it and unlocking the screen. Jacob didn't notice. I jabbed in the corner, roughly where the call icon was, and again nearer the top of the screen. There was always one person at the top of my contact list.

I waited, listening intently for the sound of the call ringing, of Aaron answering and hopefully figuring out I was in trouble. I hoped Jacob couldn't hear my phone call, but between the scuff of his feet on the dirty floor and the flapping of the tarpaulin sheets in the wind, the sound passed him by. It felt like the wind was trying to rip the roof from the house, trying to demolish it before it was even built. It whistled through the gaps around the window, enough to rustle my hair and wobble the bucket by the door. Jacob kicked it and the orange plastic vessel flew across the room, smashing into pieces on the wall beside me, dislodging a well-used trowel which fell to the ground, resting half a dozen feet away.

Jacob stopped his pacing and prickled, as if listening for something. I hastily jabbed at the phone, hoping to end the call before he heard anything, but it wasn't me he was listening for. A car was approaching. It crunched to a halt on the muddy, brick-strewn garden out front.

Jacob resumed his pacing, flicking the knife to catch my eye again, and smiled a conceited grin.

"Backup is here."

"Jacob, whatever you're planning, you're just going to make this worse. Give up now. I can help you."

"Too late."

The sound of footsteps grew as someone entered the house, using the same path we had. They scuffed on the dusty floor, searching from room to room and then climbing the stairs. Jacob held his breath as they finally approached us.

John Brandon filled the doorway, taking in the scene with wild, concerned eyes. He glanced between me and Jacob, as if he thought this was some sort of trick of the light, before his gaze settled on the glinting knife.

"Jacob," he said carefully, but his voice held nothing of the certainty I'd heard from him earlier. He spoke as if faced with a dangerous animal and even held his hands up as he slowly walked into the room, taking each step with caution.

I felt a burning hot trickle of fear run down my neck and settle on my injured shoulder. John wasn't a father about to tell his son off. He was a scared man. And if John was worried about what Jacob might do with the knife, perhaps it was time for me to start to panic too.

\* \* \*

"Have you seen Anna?" Aaron asked, poking his head through the open office door.

Jay shrugged, barely looking up from his computer, and Chris frowned back, fixing him with keen eyes. The man was like a sniper, watching and waiting for his moment.

"She's not here," Jay said. "We sent her to get lunch."

Aaron squeezed his grip around his mobile phone.

"Why?" asked Chris.

"No reason," he replied quickly, eager to get the man's attention focused on something else. "She just left me an odd voicemail. Must have been a pocket dial."

"She'll be back any minute." Jay waved his hand as he spoke. "Or she's gotten herself into one of those Crazy McArthur situations, like a mugging or a bank robbery. You know Anna."

"Yes, we do know Anna," muttered Chris, his voice dripping with sarcasm, but he still watched Aaron out the corner of his eye. "We know what she's like and we don't need any of that crap today."

Aaron turned back to the door, ready to leave this conversation behind, but a glare from Chris stopped him. The older man scrutinised him and Aaron met his gaze, keeping his face set. Though a man of few words, Chris was an expert at reading people.

"Why are you so worried about her?" he asked, keeping his voice quiet.

"I'm not," Aaron replied. "Chief Constable Price is due here any time this afternoon and I need something good to distract him with. How's the case going?"

"Helena Brandon is about to be released," said Jay, irritation curbing his words. "She's resorting to saying *no comment* to all our questions and we've got nothing more we can hold her on."

"George Cates has agreed to come in to speak about the land deal with Brandons," Chris finished. "Once we have his statement, we can take it from there. Hopefully we'll find enough to nab Helena on."

Aaron hummed but it didn't quite come out as disapproving as he was hoping. There was something in the back of his mind, tugging for his attention, something odd about that voicemail.

"That isn't enough to blind Price to the fact we've made no progress on the Ali Burgess case in the last three months."

If the mood could have been described as positive before that, then it was definitely sullen now. Aaron didn't like to keep reminding them about the threat hanging over their heads – the possibility of not closing the case in the chief constable's imaginary time frame and being subject to his whim of exerting his power – but the threat was still very much there. If they didn't get some good results soon, they'd face transfers. The Serious Crimes unit would be disbanded and the great balance they were just starting to find with Anna on the team would be lost.

At the risk of pissing everyone off, Aaron left Chris and Jay to grumble and headed back to his own office. To his surprise, Chris followed him.

"What is it?" Aaron asked as he sat down at his desk.

He left his mobile phone on the top, the little notification banner on the screen still telling him he had one missed call. But pocket-dialling wasn't really a thing nowadays, not with touchscreens, so what had Anna been doing?

Chris didn't speak. He sat down in the chair opposite Aaron's desk, his face set into a surly glare. And he waited, knowing that eventually Aaron would break the silence.

"Don't look at me like that," Aaron warned him. "I should be mad at you. You made it sound like you had a big breakthrough on this case, the lab tests confirmed the killer used the church to get rid of their bloody clothing. You should have had Helena Brandon bang to rights by now."

"She's not an easy nut to crack," Chris replied, choosing his words carefully. "She's got a solicitor who knows her stuff and they have no qualms about being uncooperative. We'll get her."

"Then why are you in here?" It wasn't like Chris to be worried but unless Aaron was mistaken, he was. He was tense, his shoulders held tightly as his hands gripped the arms of the chair.

"I'm worried about you," said Chris. "Price only comes here to dig up dirt or to lord it over us minions. And he's going to see right through you and Anna."

"What about us?"

Chris rolled his eyes. "Oh, come off it. Did you think I wasn't smart enough to catch your flirty looks, your face lighting up every time you saw her? If Price is looking to find something juicy, he's going to have a fucking party with you."

Aaron's breath stuck in his throat, like there was an invisible wall blocking his windpipe. Chris's expression of derision hadn't lessened and, if anything, his glare was willing Aaron to give away *more* than he'd already deduced.

"It's not against the rules," Aaron managed to say. "We're not doing anything wrong."

"Since when have the rules ever mattered to Price? The slightest hint of misconduct and he'll come down on us like a ton of bricks, whether it's true or not. You're just asking for him to disband us."

"I'm not." Aaron stiffened in his seat, now just as rigid as Chris.

"It's not like you to think with your dick."

"That's enough," he snapped. "With Anna, this isn't just a… I like her."

Chris held up his hands, but his shoulders relaxed a little and his frown subsided into his usual scowl.

"All right, all right. I know it's not just a fling or whatever. You seem different. Happier, I guess. My point is that we'll be bloody lucky to distract Price this afternoon when we have nothing good to wave in his face. The Ali Burgess case hasn't moved in almost a year, we're close but not close enough to pinning this murder on Helena Brandon, and now you've got a secret that could ruin your career."

Aaron sighed, feeling himself deflate like a balloon at Chris's honesty. He was usually able to dance around the obvious when speaking to the chief constable, to bore him with efficiency and statistics, but today was going to be an entirely different interaction. And unless Anna showed up all in one piece within the next hour, that odd voicemail was only going to play on his mind even more as he wondered what she was doing.

Realising Chris was waiting for some sort of acknowledgement, Aaron mumbled at him, "You're right, I guess. Like a wise old man on a mountain top."

"I prefer to think of myself as Alfred to your Batman," Chris said, giving himself a self-satisfied nod of approval.

Aaron raised an eyebrow at the man.

"My sons made me watch the new film last night," Chris said.

"Come on then, old man, how do we distract Price from the lack of progress we're making on all fronts?"

"We could blame the slow lab reports and lack of staff."

Aaron almost rolled his eyes, although that wasn't going to help the situation. "Oh yes, that will really get the chief constable in a good mood…"

"Then don't play the blame game, bore him with the positives," replied Chris with a shrug. "You'll think of something. That's why you've got the big office; you're much better at sugar-coating the bullshit than I am."

## Chapter Nineteen

For such a large and intimidating man, John Brandon was doing an expert impression of a small mouse faced with a hungry cat. I watched him freeze in place by the door, his eyes wide as he followed Jacob's movements, like he anticipated some sort of sudden reaction. I had never seen a grown man look more scared of a teenage boy. Although tall like his father, Jacob held on to his lanky figure and, if he wanted to, John could snap him in two. However, I got the distinct impression that Jacob remained in control of this situation, and John Brandon wasn't about to stand up to his son.

"She knows," Jacob said through gritted teeth as he waved the knife my way. "She found that fucking photo of me wearing my glasses. I knew we'd fucking left them behind."

"If you knew we'd left them in Yvonne's house, why didn't you say?" his father asked.

"Because it was *your* fucking job to clean up the evidence!" Jacob roared, spinning on his heels to face his dad.

John clamped his mouth shut again and took half a step back.

Looking between the two of them, I couldn't believe I was seeing such a reversal in dynamics. All along, I'd suspected Helena was the murderer, the leader who pushed people into covering up Yvonne's death. But what if it was a family affair all along?

"Why would you kill Yvonne?" I asked, taking my time to look at each of them until they met my gaze. "If you're all involved, why would you do it? What had she done to deserve that?"

Jacob waved the knife, coming very close to losing his grip on it. "Ask him!" He motioned to his father. "This is all his fault, he caused this!"

But John quickly dipped his head and avoided our gaze. I heard him sniff.

"John?" I said gently.

He sniffed again, this time sounding wetter, as though he was on the verge of tears.

"Go on, Dad, tell her!"

"I liked Yvonne," John said, his head still bent so his chin was in his chest. "We talked together. She was my friend."

"She was more than a friend, you liar!" Jacob said, spit flying through air. "Apparently marriage vows mean nothing to this piece of shit."

So, John was having an affair and Jacob found out… That still seemed like a massive overreaction on Jacob's behalf. He'd cut Yvonne's throat. Even if Jacob had inherited his mother's temper, he had committed a brutal murder and roped his parents into it too. It was too much violence for a simple affair.

I wasn't an expert, I reminded myself. No matter how many cases I worked, how many dysfunctional marriages I saw, and how many affairs were uncovered, I would never fully understand some people. As I'd learnt with Sam, anyone had the capacity to hurt another, no matter how much they supposedly loved them.

Jacob resumed his pacing of the room while his dad remained by the door. From the grumble of swear words under his breath, I guessed he was starting to realise he was running out of options.

"So, what's the plan, Jacob?" I asked, hoping to prompt his anxiety a bit more. "Because you can't keep me here forever. And you can't hurt me. My colleagues know where I am, and they'll be expecting me back any minute now. It won't be long before they come looking for me."

A small white lie, but I hoped it would work in my favour. Now I wished I hadn't gone off-plan and had told someone where I was really going. Chris was going to be so angry with me.

I couldn't tell if Jacob was in the right frame of mind to be reasoned with, but right now it was my best chance of getting out of this building site unscathed.

Jacob chewed my words over, but he didn't reply.

"Jacob, it's over," I said. "Just put down the knife and this will be over with."

"Don't tell me what to do!" he yelled, taking a sudden step towards me with the knife outstretched, its blade shining back my tense expression.

I backed away until I was against the wall.

"Jacob," John tried. He took a tentative step, attracting Jacob's fury.

"Don't speak!" Jacob warned. "I mean it, Dad, don't come any closer. Just let me think!"

Whilst Jacob squared up to his father, I took my chance. I dropped down, keeping my gaze firmly on Jacob and the knife but using my hand to feel around the gritty floor. I found the trowel just a few feet away. As far as weapons went, it wasn't as good as a knife, but it could be enough to buy me some time.

I popped it into my pocket and enclosed my hand around it, ready for the right moment. John watched me out the corner of his eye, but just as I'd suspected, he didn't say anything to Jacob. Something told me that as much as John Brandon would protect his family, he wanted this nightmare to be over with as much as I did.

John's mobile phone beeped in his pocket. Only when Jacob nodded at him, did he pull it out and read the message.

"Your mum is on her way," he said. "She's been released pending charges."

"Good," Jacob snapped back at him. "She'll know what to do. Not like you, you useless prick."

"What to do?" John asked feebly.

"With her!"

Once again, the knife found its way over to me, reflected light dancing off the surface and creating patterns on the wall.

Jacob got closer this time, close enough to press me right against the wall. I felt the cool blade against my skin, this time at the base of my neck. Jacob Brandon leaned over me. I felt a trickle of something wet down my collar and I guessed the knife had nicked me. I gripped the trowel in my pocket. The smell of blood filled the air and reminded me of Yvonne Garrington, lying dead in her kitchen. Jacob had done that to her; what would he do to me?

* * *

Aaron had left Chris grumbling about the lack of progress in order to go and get some fresh air. They were doing all they could, but it still hadn't been enough to keep Helena Brandon in custody. She'd just been released, much to Chris and Jay's annoyance, and her departure had left a sourness in the air.

Maddie appeared back in the office just before he left; she'd been roped into helping with a spate of shoplifters in the town centre for the morning, but she immediately got stuck in at Anna's desk, chasing the outstanding lab reports.

And Anna still wasn't back.

A wicked wind was rising up and whipping the trees around the station into a frenzy, creating a low, constant roar. Hidden in the shadows of the building, just out of sight from the main entrance, Aaron hoped that he would stay undisturbed as he fumbled in his pocket for a cigarette and light. He saw a familiar sleek Jag slink into the car park as he lit up and watched his first exhaled breath whisk away on the breeze. Chief Constable Price, right on time.

The car parked up and its smooth engine cut. Aaron watched as the man got out, straightened his suit jacket and headed straight over to him, joining him under the broken security camera at the far end of the station premises. Without a word, Price leant against the wall and Aaron felt compelled to offer him a fag. He accepted it and carefully avoided Aaron's gaze with a penchant look across the horizon.

"One of those days, is it?" he asked, brandishing the cigarette. "Filthy habit. My missus will bend my ear when I get home. I only smoke when I'm drinking."

"Me too," Aaron replied. "Or stressed," he added. Since it was too early to be drinking, today must have fallen under the latter.

Every silence with Chief Constable Price felt like a pressure, like he was waiting for a fanfare of thanks for showing his face. Aaron couldn't stomach that today, and he was barely able to manage an acceptable level of fawning anyway. Pressed to fill the quiet, he scrambled for something to say.

Price beat him to it, however.

"You know it's illegal to smoke on police property."

Aaron almost laughed. Of all the people wanting to spout on about the rules, it was him. Aaron knew the man was the biggest hypocrite on the force; he advocated for strict standards for police officers, but he didn't uphold those values for himself or his own lackeys.

"Then arrest me," said Aaron, earning a chuckle from the chief constable.

"Right, I'm hoping you've got good news for me today." Price stiffened as a particularly fierce gust raced across the car park. "I would hate to waste a journey all the way over to this backwater town for nothing."

And so it began. Price could have easily just called or emailed for an update, but no, he had to show his face. He had to remind everyone, especially Aaron, of his importance, his power. He appeared particularly keen to stir up some trouble lately, well, slightly keener than usual.

Price signalled his disapproval when Aaron didn't reply.

"Nothing?"

"Not nothing," said Aaron. "The station is efficient as always, overtime is within budget, arrest rates are steadily rising. The Serious Crimes team are making good progress with the murder case of Yvonne Garrington. They're closing in."

"I hope you're taking the Ali Burgess case just as seriously. I gave you six months to find the perpetrator and get them off the streets. You've already had three."

"The case has gone cold," Aaron replied, not that he needed to point it out. It was always in the background, resources were always working away, but it was the case that just wouldn't close. After the night Anna was stabbed, the killer got away, and there had been no sign of them since. Ali Burgess was buried but her murderer continued to walk free.

Sometimes that was just how it went.

"Cold," Price said with a snort. "You want to stick to that? Because I made it clear what happens to the Serious Crimes team if that is the case. I still get asked by people even more important than me why haven't we found who committed that horrific murder yet. I don't like not having an answer for them."

"I know what you said." Aaron remembered the threat well. "Unless new evidence comes to light, we won't be able to close the case, not in a month, or three, or any time frame you decide to set."

That wasn't the answer Price wanted. Aaron reminded himself of the one rule he had with the chief constable – *just agree*. It was easier, safer, to just agree with him and get him out of the way. Everything worked so much better when he was at head office and Aaron was left to run King's Lynn on his own.

Once upon a time, he dreamed of going far in his career, maybe even all the way up to the top, but with Price at the helm, that wasn't going to happen. So, it was better for everyone if he just bit his tongue, nodded along and waited for Price to leave him alone.

Price opened his mouth to speak but he was cut off by the abrupt ring of Aaron's mobile phone. Aaron dropped his cigarette and crushed it underfoot as he fished the device from his pocket. Its shrillness was piercing, even dampened by the roaring wind, as though the phone somehow knew how urgent the call was.

"Where are you?" came Maddie's pumped voice from the other end.

"Talking with Chief Constable Price," Aaron replied curtly.

"Oh." Maddie took a moment to measure the sharpness in his reply. "Well, please come to the office if you can, *sir*," she said, elongating the last word. "I've made a breakthrough."

"What breakthrough?"

At these words, Aaron straightened up and Price cocked his head. He too dropped his cigarette and stood on the butt as he listened intently.

"The lab recovered DNA from the glasses at the scene. No direct match but they did flag a familial match to someone who already had their details and DNA in the database… Helena Brandon."

"A familial match?"

"Half match," Maddie explained. "So, a child. Jacob."

In the background of the call, Aaron heard the scrape of the desk chairs on the floor and the scrabble of people moving.

"Chris and Jay want to bring him in now."

"Tell them to wait," said Aaron. "I'm on my way."

## Chapter Twenty

Aaron hoped that having spent years behind a desk, blagging his way to the top command, meant that Chief Constable Price wouldn't be as quick on his feet as he was. He *really* hoped that was the case when he bounded up the stairs ahead of the big boss and heard Jay's voice floating clearly along the corridor from the Serious Crimes office.

"Wait, so they're like… together? As in, just shagging, or is he actually head over heels for her?"

Chris hissed back. "If you were any sort of detective, you would have figured that out by now like I did."

Jay's voice turned incredulous. "I can't believe you *both* knew. For how long?"

The speculation stopped abruptly when Aaron entered the office. Chris, Jay and Maddie froze in place, all in various states of getting ready to leave the office. Footsteps on the metal stairwell preceded Price as he lagged behind.

"Where's Anna?"

The question just fell from Aaron's mouth, bypassing his brain completely. A quick glance at Price revealed he was now stood in the office doorway with a frown on his face, not understanding the urgency.

No one seemed to feel the same urgency that he did.

"Don't know," Maddie replied. "Jay just tried calling her but she's still not answering. She's been gone over an hour now."

Aaron bit his lip as he risked a glance at Chris. The older detective's face hardened as he gritted his teeth together, reading Aaron like a book. He knew exactly what he was thinking.

"I know where she's gone," Chris said. "Given the chance, I bet she's gone to speak to Reverend Harding. Or worse, Jacob Brandon."

"She wouldn't," said Jay, looking around the room and seeking out someone just as confused as he was. "Would she?"

"You said it yourself; she's probably got herself into some sort of Crazy McArthur situation," replied Aaron. "If it's going to happen, it'll happen to Anna."

Finally, the urgency, irritating and relentless, started to infect the others too. Maddie found her car keys, jingling them in her hand as she waited for instructions. Jay looked between Chris and Aaron, carefully avoiding Chief Constable Price, who seemed to be enjoying being an observer.

"What do we know about Jacob Brandon? Is he violent?" Aaron asked, hoping the bit of extra information might kickstart his brain into thinking of some next steps.

"Possibly," Jay replied. "We haven't got much on him, but he hangs around with Brady Boston."

Maddie pursed her lips. "That little gobshite isn't above that sort of behaviour."

"And we know his mother has a temper on her," concluded Jay.

It was a start. Aaron fought the urge to look at Price directly, to see just how derisive the chief constable's expression was.

"Get your coat, you're coming with us," Chris barked at Aaron, making Maddie jump with the sharpness in his voice.

"Why?" Aaron asked.

"Because if Anna's gone against my orders like I think she has, she's in big trouble," came the answer. "Come on, Batman, let's go find a murderer."

\* \* \*

This was turning into a family affair, and I got the distinct impression the Brandon family were the type to do anything to hide their secrets. Even murder. Once Helena arrived, only slightly dishevelled from her night at the police station, Jacob's frantic pacing stopped. John cowered, like a servant afraid of his master. It took Helena less than a second to assess the situation as she pushed her husband aside to enter the room. She threw a dirty look my way but rested her gaze on her son, her expression turning to pity.

"Honey, are you okay?"

Her innocent, sweet voice made me feel sick. I was sitting, leaning against the wall after getting tired of standing. Jacob tensed whenever I tried to look at my watch, but I guessed I had been in the half-built room for over an hour now. The wind had disturbed enough of the dust and plasterboards to coat my clothes in a fine layer, and a tickly cough was irritating my lungs. The trowel was in my pocket, its rough edges sticking into my hip.

Jacob sniffed, struggling to suck in air through his gritted teeth as he pouted at his mum. "She knows. She's got the photograph from the community centre board of me wearing my glasses."

Helena's evil glare turned on me. "Oh."

I jumped as a buzzing interrupted her and caused her gaze to flare at me. Cautiously, well aware of the relentless disturbance coming from my pocket, I rose to my feet and held my mobile out for them to see Jay's name across the screen as the call remained unanswered.

"I told you my colleagues would be looking for me," I said to Jacob. "Stop this now, or it's only going to get worse."

My words did appear to sway Jacob a little as he paused and looked at his mother, waiting for her reaction. After a moment of consideration, Helena stepped forward to me and snatched the phone. She dropped it to the ground and stood on the screen with her sensible heel.

With a crunch and crack, the buzzing stopped.

"There," she said triumphantly. "No more colleagues to worry about. In fact…"

She strode over to me with far more confidence than she deserved and dived into my pocket, pulling out the picture of Jacob from the community centre noticeboard. Thankfully, she missed the trowel in my other pocket, but I couldn't let that small relief show as she held the photo in front of me and tore it into dozens of pieces. She let the pieces rain down to the ground and the wind whipped them across the room.

"There. Now no more evidence either," she said.

"You're insane," I spat back. "Even if you figure out how to keep me quiet, there's plenty of evidence implicating you all. We have the glasses; we can link them to Jacob."

"You might have his glasses," Helena said, retreating back to Jacob, "but you have no physical proof my son was there. At the moment, you have nothing to link any of us to Yvonne's death."

She settled into the crook of her son's body and placed her arm around his waist. A shiver ran through me at their closeness, at how comfortable and smug they looked together. They were two halves of a whole; two sides of the mirror. A mother-son murdering team.

"So, Detective McArthur," she said.

She wasn't fazed by the knife in Jacob's hand, or the way he gripped it so tightly his knuckles were white. She wasn't bothered by her husband, stood by the door, almost blending into the shadows and offering no help to anyone. She just delighted in facing me.

"Let's discuss what we're going to do with you. You see, Yvonne might have been a terrible mistake, but it made me realise just how far I would go to protect my family. And I won't let some jumped-up junior detective like you ruin my family's future."

Jacob straightened up at his mother's words, a cruel smile crossing his face. He flexed, eager, with hungry eyes watching me, as if daring me to try and run. He'd catch me quickly with his dad blocking the door. And from the way he held the shiny chrome knife, I knew he wanted to use it.

I gripped the trowel in my pocket, feeling its plaster-covered surfaces under my fingers. It was no match for the shiny knife.

Damn it. I had no chance.

"Helena," came a quiet, uncertain voice by the door, as if testing the waters.

Helena rounded on her husband, her face flashing thunder.

"What, John? You want us to go easy on her? Don't forget, this is all your fault. Whatever sob story you spun to Yvonne about your life, all of this has happened because of you. Be thankful Jacob and I have covered up this mess, rather than leaving you to take the fall. You're the one who caused this, not us!"

John shrank back into the shadows, shying away from his wife like a dog with its tail between its legs.

A great gust of wind tore at the plastic sheet covering the window, ripping it from its fastenings. Everyone flinched as the breeze flicked up more dust, covering me in a shower of fine grit and making me cough until I could taste the plasterboard fibres. My glimpse outside revealed a grey-skied world, with thick clouds threatening to burst, and I knew I couldn't sit around any longer. The more time the Brandons had to think this through, the more dangerous they became. They were smart people, and I had no doubt they would go to great lengths to stop me from revealing what I'd found out.

I thumbed the trowel. I had to figure a way out of this soon.

With an indignant spit, Helena dusted herself off. "Ridiculously filthy place. I need to go get clean; I can still feel that disgusting police station on my skin."

She untangled herself from her son and headed for the door, John hastily moving out of her way.

"Oh, and, Jacob," she said as she paused by her husband, her back to him. A bemused smile tugged at her bitchy face as she wagged a finger at him. "Try not to make a mess, darling. That's a new jacket. Your father will help you clear up."

And with that, she stomped downstairs in her mud-covered heels. I listened with bated breath until her footsteps faded away and the sound of an engine signalled her leaving the building site. I was now back to where I'd started; with a maniacal teenage knifeman and his accomplice father.

I was running out of time before they made a move.

The wind smashed into the house once again; it loosened half a dozen more of the fastenings around the plastic sheet at the window and tugged the tarpaulin into the room, where it swished like underwater seaweed in a strong tide. The sudden gust made Jacob jump and for a brief moment, I saw his grip on the knife lessen and the colour return to his knuckles.

Now was as good as any other time.

I pulled the trowel out and launched myself at him, managing to knock him off balance and send him tumbling to the ground. He held on to the knife well, until I landed on top of him and jabbed at his wrist with the trowel, causing raw lacerations on his pasty skin. His fingers recoiled and I took the chance to kick the knife away. It landed among the pieces of the broken bucket.

I didn't have time to take stock as I leapt to my feet again and propelled myself to the door. John Brandon still stood there, obscured by the shadows. But he made no move as I approached and even swayed back a step with a gentle push, allowing me to pass. Soon, I was off down the stairs and out of the house, just as I heard Jacob make it to his feet and scream at his father.

"Don't just stand there, you useless shit. Get her!"

## Chapter Twenty-One

"Are you all right?" Maddie asked, watching the expression on Aaron's face. After a small debate in which Aaron had ignored everything that Price suggested, he'd joined Maddie and set off to the community centre at St Mary's Church whilst Chris and Jay headed for the Brandon household. Uniformed officers were also being dispatched to the local area to help find Jacob Brandon, but the team were keen not to spook the lad.

As he got out of Maddie's patrol car, Aaron slammed the door closed a little too hard, which only heightened her interest in his mood.

"Fine," he answered quickly, pushing down any worry before it made it to the surface. "There's Anna's car."

The rusty pile of scrap metal that belonged to Anna was parked across from the community centre, however, there was no sign of her or anyone else around. The only movement on the street was the oak leaves being hassled along the road by the relentless wind.

Maddie moved over to the community centre building, trying the door. Tearing his gaze away from the car, Aaron scanned the surrounding area, and then once more for good measure, all the while calling Anna's number. It repeatedly rang out, as though her phone wasn't even on. It wasn't beyond the realm of possibility that Anna had let the battery die. Regardless, her phone wasn't in the car, but a quick try of the handle showed the car was unlocked with her keys and warrant card inside. Aaron tutted to himself.

"You look worried," Maddie observed as she made her way back to him.

"I'm not. Any other places we should look?" Aaron asked, keen to get Maddie's prying gaze off him.

"There's a den behind the building," she replied, pointing. "And the victim's house is down there. I'll go check the house."

Sharing a nod, they parted ways, just as Aaron's phone began to ring. But it was only Chris.

"They're not here," said the surly detective down the line, somehow sounding more irritated than he was before. "The Brandon's house is locked up tight, no one home."

"We've got Anna's car," said Aaron, "it's here at the community centre. No sign of her, though. Where are the other likely places for the Brandons to go? They can't have just vanished."

"The son sometimes hangs out with his friends behind the community centre."

"I'm looking there now." Faced with an overgrown hedge thickened with brambles, Aaron tried to make out the entrance to the den. What a day to wear his nicest suit. Nevertheless, he pushed through the undergrowth until he emerged on the empty den.

"No one here," he reported, although it looked like it hadn't been long since the den was occupied. A half-empty can of cheap beer sat on a table made of wooden pallets. Large, rough splinters held it upright in the bracing wind. "Put out details of their cars countywide and share them with Cambridgeshire too, just in case they're thinking of doing a runner. Have we got someone checking the boy's school?"

"We do, Jay's on it now," Chris confirmed gruffly.

"Get a unit posted to their house in case they return."

"On it," replied Chris and he ended the call.

Aaron stood still and listened for a while, focusing on the howl of the wind as it forced its way through the small gaps in the hedge and the outside of the community centre. It was building in his head, preventing all other sounds from reaching him and all other thoughts from focusing his mind. He stalked the small den, checking once more for any clues, then turned to leave. But before he braced himself to push back through the brambly hedge, Aaron kicked out at the makeshift table. The structure collapsed into pieces and the beer can tumbled to the ground, spilling its fizzy contents onto the leaf-strewn ground. However, it didn't make him feel any better.

\* \* \*

My feet pounded on the asphalt as I escaped from the house, heading in the direction of the looming church tower and hopefully to my car. As I crossed the threshold of the street to the shadowed alleyway, I heard Jacob stumble from the house behind me. If John was also following, he was much slower or much stealthier.

The alleyway took me past the six-foot high fences of some back gardens, all being showered in a persistent rain of falling leaves. The stone wall of the churchyard was just ahead, and I knew beyond that was the community centre and my car. The sodden leaves made the pavements slippery and as I avoided what I thought was a particularly thick patch, I skidded on another. I landed ungracefully, managing to save myself with the palm of my hands. But the fall cost me time and when I looked back, Jacob was already in the alleyway.

The knife looked heavy in his hands, lumbering him as he sprinted down with his spindly legs pumping hard. Tiny flecks of blood dropped on the ground from where I'd grazed him with the trowel. I jumped back up, ignoring the mud and leaves stuck to my front now, and legged it as fast as I could. I heard Jacob's breath as he neared, even felt the wind change as his presence grew closer.

The end of the alleyway was in sight. I spied a vehicle at the entrance to the car park, Battenburg markings reflecting even in the dim daylight. But it was just too far for me to reach.

Something caressed my neck and Jacob took hold of my collar. He pulled me and I fell to the ground once again, this time landing flat on my back. I rolled to the side just in time as the knife came down from above, slashing at my face.

I kicked out at Jacob, landing a good one to his knee. He stumbled, giving me just enough time to get back to my feet. With the end of the alley too far, the wind too loud to be heard over, and my attacker too fast for me to outrun, I vaulted over the church wall that sat behind me, landing in a muddy patch of grass in the churchyard.

I knew I couldn't stop; Jacob would be right behind me. I dodged between the gravestones, weaving in an unknown pattern and hoping inspiration might come to me as I made it to one of the great oak trees swaying dangerously in the wind. Its trunk creaked and groaned with the effort. On the other side lay the church. I was the wrong side of the building to get to the car park and the police car. But I was fairly close to the door.

The knife struck the tree just above my head, embedding deep in the bark. I ducked and felt a trickle down my scalp. Sap? Jacob appeared next to me, his hand still on the knife handle, and he tugged to get it loose. I pushed myself off the trunk and ran for the door.

The church had a solid wooden door with an ancient lock, and I hadn't exactly thought about how I would get through that until I reached it. But someone had beaten me to it. John Brandon stood up straight as he spotted me, and as he did, the door to the church clicked unlocked. The wind pushed the door inwards, creating a ghostly scream as it whistled through the gap. I started to back away, but John grabbed my arm. With a tight grip and effortless pull, he dragged me into the church and slammed the door behind me.

"Jacob!" I heard him call, and his son's footsteps grew louder. "I've got her! In here!"

"You fucker!" I shouted at the door, before remembering where I was. The Brandons might not have had many qualms about killing in a church, but at that moment, I didn't want to take the chance of pissing off the owner of the house. There was a good chance this was going to end up being my final resting place.

I backed away quickly as I heard Jacob reach his father, and the door started to creak again as it opened. Left or right? If I ran towards the altar, I would have more room, but I would be truly trapped. If I ran for the back of the church, I would have even less room to escape.

Jacob and John Brandon filled the arched doorway and the wind ripped the door from their grip. Jacob strode on ahead of his dad, wielding the knife once again. He slashed at the air.

"You shouldn't have stuck your nose in," he growled as he approached. "This is family business."

I headed towards the back of the church. With me surrounded, Jacob advanced at a much slower rate.

"Don't bother hiding," he said, his voice echoing off the high ceiling, "there's nowhere to go."

It was true, there wasn't. All there was at the back of the church was a small cupboard that housed a boiler, the fireplace where we'd found the evidence, and a mass of ancient, thick velvet curtains to hide a collection of old furniture and supplies – a hoover, a stack of wooden chairs, an old lectern, boxes of candles, and a thick, woven rope tied around a hook on the wall.

The bell.

I pulled hard on the rope, surprised at how resistant it was. It took my whole body to pull it enough to shift the bell far up in the tower above me, but eventually I heard it ring with a welcoming chime. I pulled again and again, making the song louder until it rattled my brain inside my skull. It drowned out the wind, my pumping heartbeat, and Jacob's approaching footsteps.

His knife slashed at the curtain, ripping through it like butter. I ducked again but too late, and as the curtain tumbled around me, Jacob's free hand grabbed my arm. He pulled me from the recess of the church and threw me to the ground, where I landed on the stone floor with a heavy grunt. The floor was icy cold on my burning skin but worse was the shadow that Jacob cast as he loomed over me. The knife shined above me, ready to come down, and a desperate, devilish snarl tugged his lips. The room grew darker as I watched the knife, waiting for it to descend. I braced myself. I knew this feeling; I knew it bloody hurt. I knew what was coming.

"Stop!" shouted a voice, firm and commanding.

Jacob paused. And when he looked up, the rabid fury on his face disappeared with a dying growl.

I looked round. Standing in the aisle between the pews at the back of the church was Maddie, adopting a stable stance as she held her taser out, pointing right at Jacob. And just between the pews towards the door, I spied

Aaron barking orders at John Brandon to get on the ground, whilst holding Maddie's baton.

As the red dots danced over Jacob's torso, he let go of the knife and it clattered to the stone floor beside me, echoing through the church and up into the vaulted ceiling above us.

## Chapter Twenty-Two

I was a dab hand at first aid. I'd patched myself and other people up enough over the years that I considered whether I should move careers and become a paramedic. Although as police, we did sometimes get roped into performing life-saving first aid in extreme circumstances. In my second year on the job, I responded first to a desperate 999 call from a mother whose child was choking. I performed CPR until the proper medics arrived and the child was taken to hospital, and after that, I never heard from them again. I didn't know how the boy was, if he made it, I didn't hear what had happened to cause the accident or how his mother was coping. That was one of the best parts about switching to detective work – it gave me a bit more closure. I didn't like not knowing how things ended. And, like skipping to the end of a book, I grabbed every chance I had at closure.

I watched Chris and Jay from the observation room, secretly pleased I wasn't in the interviews with them, where tempers were fraying. They were determined to get to the end of this case too, to nail the charges on this family and finally answer the question of who killed Yvonne Garrington and why. And I was determined to watch this until the end.

The Brandons were not making it easy, however.

They had started with John, who didn't say a word. Helena had spent a long time conferring with the solicitor, enough time for Chris to tell me off for my actions. And now, Chris and Jay were having a go at Jacob.

Aaron entered the observation room and settled next to me without a word. I saw him glance at my posture, noting how I held a bundle of bandages to the top of my head. The sap I had assumed was running down my hair was actually blood from where Jacob had nicked me with the knife by the tree. It wasn't bad though, and with a bit of pressure it was easing. Aaron handed me a cup of steaming coffee and, with a tight smile, he wiggled my hand free from the bandage and took over pressing it down.

"Chief Constable Price wants to talk to you," he said before taking a long sip of his own coffee.

I hummed back in acknowledgement and quickly decided I would worry about that later.

"Has he copped to it yet?" Aaron nodded towards the interviewee.

"Not yet," I replied. "Chris and Jay are trying their best."

"I don't quite understand one thing though," said Aaron, waiting for me to shoot him a quizzical look before continuing. "Did the boy really kill Yvonne just because his dad was having an affair with her? Slit her throat for that?"

"No," I murmured back and inhaled a deep breath of air tinged with strong coffee. "I think he killed her because she saw what he really was. She knew he was a monster."

Before Aaron could respond, a bang from the interview room distracted us. Jacob Brandon slammed his hands on the table.

"They're not my glasses!" he declared, a flare of anger appearing underneath his moody teenage glare. Beside him sat Melanie Georgiou and, on the other side, the designated appropriate adult.

"They had your DNA on," Jay pointed out and he tapped at the lab report on the table between them.

Jacob was using the tactic of shouting over the truth, the slightly more mature version of sticking one's fingers in their ears and singing *la-la-la*. It wasn't going to work with Chris and Jay, who had enough patience between them to wait out the silly games, although I wondered just how strong that patience really was.

Melanie Georgiou was losing her rag; she didn't have much of a leg to stand on and she knew it. "My client is a minor; we don't consent to the use of their DNA for this purpose."

"It's a murder investigation," said Jay. "Nice try but that's not how it works. That defence also won't work when our application for Jacob's medical records comes through and we can see if the glasses we hold in our evidence locker match his prescription. Or when we piece together the photograph that Detective McArthur found of you wearing said glasses. They're your glasses, Jacob, and we can prove it."

Jacob started to object, his voice rising higher until it was just noise, and Georgiou vainly tried to disarm with legal jargon. They both fell silent when Chris thumped his fist on the table.

"Look," he said, his voice taking on a scary and serious edge. "We're not in the mood for this dancing around anymore. We know you went to Yvonne Garrington's house that night after rehearsals. You can deny it all you want, but it would be better for your whole family if you finally started to give us the truth."

I had my fingers crossed. I knew that if they really wanted to, the Brandons could drag this investigation out further; the burden was on us to find the evidence that proved exactly which one of them killed Yvonne.

"All right, fine," Jacob said, slouching back in his chair, a perfect picture of an insolent teenager. "Those are my glasses."

"Jacob, I suggest you stop talking," Melanie Georgiou said through her gritted teeth.

"What's the point?" Jacob threw her a hateful look. "You know we're cooked; they know we're cooked! I went to see Yvonne that night after the concert rehearsal."

"Why?" Chris asked, pushing forward before the solicitor could interrupt.

"She wouldn't stop looking at Dad. They'd been working together on this deal, and he'd been sleeping with her, because he's a sad, lonely fuck. He even went to see her that day, right before rehearsals." The lad gagged with disgust.

Jay leaned forwards, catching Jacob's gaze. "You knew your dad and Yvonne were having an affair?"

Jacob rolled his shoulders, looking away in a flash. "I suppose, if you want to call old-people sex that. Yvonne said that Dad had told her what their marriage was really like. All the arguments and fights. She felt sorry for him, and she wanted to help. That night, at the rehearsals, she told me she knew what it was like to be trapped in a bad marriage and she didn't want to see anyone else suffer like she had. She was going to speak up."

Jacob sat back in a dreamy haze as he stared at Chris and Jay with an expression of someone seeing daylight for the first time.

"She told you this?" Jay asked.

Jacob nodded and wrinkled his nose. "Like she thought she was doing me a favour. She thought, by separating my mum and dad, that she was saving our family. She wanted to ruin their marriage to *save me*, ruin my family! I went to her that night, tried to tell her she was wrong, but…"

"I think–" started Georgiou, although Chris silenced her with a look.

"But what?" urged Jay.

Jacob glanced at the two detectives opposite him. "She didn't listen. She wouldn't listen. She just sat there at the kitchen table, drinking her tea, thinking she could tell everyone about *my* family… So, I… I found one of her knives on the worktop."

"And then what happened?"

"Jacob," warned Georgiou, although it fell on deaf ears.

"I just saw red; I was so angry. I had the knife…" Jacob bared his teeth and threw his arm out in a sideways motion, a slash as if holding a knife out. "It shut her up. I forgot all about my glasses. I must have dropped them…"

A heavy silence fell over the interview room. Chris and Jay let Jacob stew for a moment, reliving the night in question in his mind. Just as the pressure reached boiling point, Chris leaned forwards over the table.

"So, Jacob, you admit to killing Yvonne?"

The young lad swallowed hard. "She… she was going to tell everyone."

A stir from the person next to him drew everyone's attention away from the seething teen.

Melanie Georgiou cleared her throat. "If you detectives can excuse me a moment, I have a prepared statement that might shed some more light on this."

Even with their backs to me, I caught Chris and Jay exchange a look of concern.

"From Jacob?" asked Chris, although the lad was scowling too.

"No," replied the solicitor. "From his mother."

With another look at Jay and a slight frown, Chris waved for her to go on. The solicitor produced a neatly folded note from her leather-bound book, unfurling it with care, and cleared her throat again.

"I, Helena Brandon, take full responsibility for the death of Yvonne Garrington. I know my son, Jacob, will want to protect me and so will give a false testimony that he was her killer, but it is untrue. I had my son's glasses in my pocket at the time I visited Yvonne at her home, and most likely dropped them. I do not consent to any further interviews of my son, nor to his continued detainment during this investigation."

Beside me, Aaron whistled under his breath, and his hand pushing on the bandage twitched on top of my head. A quick glance round at him showed a deep scowl across his face.

"That's a dirty trick," he said quietly. "Last resort."

I sucked in a breath through my gritted teeth. "You see why I don't like solicitors now."

From the little expression I could see of Jay and Chris, they were as unimpressed with this admission as Aaron.

"For fuck's sake," said Jay and he slumped back in his chair.

\* \* \*

It took until early evening before the bleeding from the small cut on my scalp finally stopped. Aaron tried to suggest going to the hospital to get it glued together but he didn't put up much of a fight when I refused. I wanted to get this chat with Chief Constable Price over and done with before I left the station so he could return back to head office and leave the team alone. And from his awkwardness, I could tell Aaron wanted the chief to bugger off too.

Chief Constable Price had set up camp in Aaron's office, which was growing dark as the night descended over the West Norfolk fields surrounding the police station. With a terse greeting he waved me to take a seat opposite his.

"All right, McArthur?" the chief constable asked, eyes flitting to the blood dried into my hair.

"Yes, sir," I replied. Despite trying my absolute best to sound positive and cool, Price's scowl only deepened at my expression.

"I'm disappointed that we are having this chat once again, McArthur. I don't like repeating myself, so I don't need to tell you again how improper it is for you to ignore orders and go running off, doing your own thing rather than pulling your weight in a case."

I opened my mouth, about to state that I wouldn't describe my actions that way, but as more of a detour than a flagrant disregard of orders. But I knew I was going to have a hard enough time convincing Chris of that, let alone the chief, so what arguments I had were never going to work. I closed my mouth again and nodded.

"For some strange reason, DCI Burns seems determined to keep you around. I suggested he get rid of you after the last incident, but he didn't. Why is that?"

Price's gaze left me and drifted to the window and the wild weather outside, illuminated by the dim street lights from the car park and road. Our reflections on the dark glass watched us back.

"I don't know, sir," I replied.

He was fishing for something, waiting for a slight reaction from me. Whatever inkling he had, he was determined to wait until I gave away what I was hiding.

He narrowed his gaze. "Are you sure there isn't something else?"

"Like what?"

"I don't know. But I do know that complicated relationships between colleagues have caused problems in the past. Cases can be compromised. I know how easy it is to fall into that trap with the nature of our jobs; the lack of people around who understand the exact nuances of what we see day in and day out. How easy it is to fall into bed with someone you shouldn't…"

I felt my face flush. I was not about to admit falling into bed with anyone to Chief Constable Price. But denying it would be outright lying, a quality frowned upon in this profession. However, under Price's scrutinising glare – his thick eyebrows pulling together as he waited just a fraction too long for my answer – I had no other choice.

"There isn't anything between Aaron and I, sir. I can assure you."

Price watched me, scrutinising every inch of my expression and posture. Eventually he relaxed, although I was under no illusion that I was out of the woods yet. He rose from the desk steadily and straightened his jacket, not bothering to look at me anymore as he slowly made for the door.

"I don't like liars on my force, McArthur. And I don't like officers who think they know better. If I get one more whiff that you've gone against orders or done anything else to pull this force into disrepute, I'll have your job. Understand?"

I gulped hard but quickly nodded when his pressing gaze fell back onto me. "Yes, sir."

"Burns won't be able to cover for you forever."

And, without another word, he left. The door closed behind him with a reverberating thud, shaking within my chest. I took a moment to breathe deeply, steadying my heart which had started going crazy.

I must have relished in silence for a while as the next thing I knew, the room was completely dark as night took a hold, and the door creaked open with caution.

After a quick pause to turn on the light, Aaron slid into the room.

"How did it go?" he asked, strolling up to me.

He had his coat on, ready to go home, I guessed. It had been a long day. I shrank down into my seat; for the first time that day, tiredness tugged at me, beckoning me to close my eyes for a short while.

"About as well as you can imagine," I replied. "He thinks you're covering for me."

Aaron thought for a moment. "Price thinks I'm covering up lots of things. He's been looking for an excuse to get rid of me for years."

"Why's that?"

Aaron waved his hand. "That's not important now." He shoved his hands deep into his coat pocket but made no other move. He just watched me, shuffling from one foot to the other until I sat up and gave him a frown.

"Are you going home?"

"Not yet." He shook his head. "I wanted to talk to you about something."

"What?"

He didn't reply. Instead, he chewed his bottom lip and fiddled with something in his pocket.

"You're not doing a lot of talking," I pointed out.

"Okay," he said, although the word was more of an assurance for himself than a response for me. He took a full breath, releasing it from his lungs as he pulled out his hand and offered me something small and metallic. "I've had this in my pocket for almost a week and I've been waiting for the right time to give it to you, but there'll probably never be a right time. Here… It's the spare key to my house."

"Are you sure?" A dozen questions entered my mind, and I fought back the urge to fire them at Aaron. Why now? Did this mean he wanted to move forward? Or was this just for convenience?

Aaron smiled at me, almost amused as he watched me attempting to bite my tongue and figure out what to say. "I am. And… well, thanks, for being patient with me."

"We don't have to do anything you're not comfortable with," I said. "I know you want to take things slow."

"There's a difference between taking things slow and not taking them anywhere at all. This seems right."

I took the key from his hands, briefly sensing his boiling-hot skin against mine, and I felt a smile break out on my face. It ached after a moment, reminding me how tired I was and how close I had come to an unwanted liaison with a knife. But still, it was progress, and I couldn't have been happier that he was really trying to make this work, just for me.

"But I need you to do something for me," said Aaron, offering a guilty look as the smile dropped from my face.

"What?"

"Jay and Chris aren't having a lot of luck with the Brandons. We need you to talk to John. You might just be able to get through to him."

## Chapter Twenty-Three

John Brandon slunk into the interview room, just a shade of the man I had met that first night at the choir concert a week ago. Melanie Georgiou followed and took the seat next to him at the table opposite Chris and me. She curled her lips as she regarded us both, landing on me and my dishevelled appearance. I marvelled at how composed she still looked despite knowing that at least one of her clients was guilty of murder even with her attempts to muddy the waters. This interview with John Brandon was my last-ditch attempt to gleam a little more information. Chris was keen to do it just because he knew it would annoy Melanie Georgiou.

"I hope for your sake that there has been more evidence found," the solicitor said with a testing sigh. She glanced at me, about to ask why I looked like I'd been dragged through a muddy puddle and had blood in my hair, but she chose not to.

"No new evidence," I replied with a shake of my head.

I looked to Chris and he nodded back, a sign to carry on. If we couldn't get the truth from Jacob or Helena, both keen to pervert the course of justice, then maybe we could get it from John. Maybe he needed someone who understood him, just a little.

"We're here because I'd like to talk to Mr Brandon about *why* Yvonne Garrington was killed."

I set my gaze on John but his remained on the floor. Next to him, Georgiou snorted and tapped her pen impatiently.

"Helena Brandon has confessed to the murder of Yvonne Garrington. Mr Brandon has nothing else to say."

I grimaced, ignoring the solicitor. "No, I don't think that's right. Because if Jacob is to be believed, John struck up a friendship with Yvonne and lied to her about the state of his marriage to garner sympathy. So, is that true, John? Did you lie to Yvonne about how poor your relationship is?"

John didn't move a muscle, head bent down as if in prayer. Under the shadows, I could see his bottom lip shaking.

I knew I wouldn't get anything from him this way. John Brandon wouldn't open up after twenty years of being downtrodden and controlled by his wife. To break through, I would have to try a different approach.

"I had a boyfriend." As I spoke, Melanie Georgiou opened her mouth, ready to ask what on earth I was on about, but Chris silenced her with a wave of his hand. I continued, speaking only to John, hoping my words might provoke a reaction. "I didn't realise at the time – probably because I was a teenager and completely infatuated with him – that he was so controlling. I couldn't go out without him; I lost all my friends. I was trapped. People who know me now wouldn't believe I ever stayed with someone like that, I'm not someone who can be pushed around so easily now. But back then, I was young and I couldn't see a way out. I fantasised about one, I dreamed of being happy without him, but I couldn't get out. I thought that perhaps that was my lot in life, that I was happy really, I was just ungrateful for what I had."

John's lip stopped quivering as he listened to me talk.

"From what I've learnt about Yvonne, I believe she felt the same way when she was married to Keith. Neither of them seemed happy but they stuck together for many years because that was what they knew. That was all they knew. Yvonne stayed with Keith because she didn't believe she deserved better, she didn't know how to be with anyone else, and really, life was just easier with him. Until he left her. Then suddenly she was on her own and, after a little while, she learned she loved it. She became a new woman, despite the problems he left behind with money. She found happiness.

"I found happiness too. It took me a while, for a long time I didn't realise the damage it had done. I don't blame Yvonne for wanting to share that happiness with the people she thought were trapped too. If what Jacob said is true, Yvonne believed you were like her; someone who dreamed of getting out of the trap but couldn't see how to."

I could have carried on, offered a bit more of the story until it really resonated with John Brandon, but John let out a whimper. His fingers started to shake.

"Do you ever feel trapped by Helena, John?"

The moment he nodded his head, Melanie Georgiou snapped at me.

"That's emotional manipulation," she said. "You're putting words into my client's mouth."

"The only emotional manipulation here is from Helena Brandon," I replied. "John, did you tell Yvonne about how bad your life at home with Helena is?"

A sob escaped as he risked a glance at me. I returned his look with a kind smile. Despite all he had done; despite trapping me in the church and helping his family cover up Yvonne's murder, he deserved a chance at redemption.

"John, I think I know what happened that night. I think you had struck up a relationship with Yvonne, and at some point during the rehearsal, she told Jacob her plan to save you from your marriage. So, he followed her home. Someone in your family held that knife and killed Yvonne, and I don't think it was you. But both your son and your wife are maintaining that they killed her, possibly to protect each other. Who is protecting you, John?"

"No one." I wasn't sure I had heard John speak at all, his voice no more than a squeak, but Georgiou huffed and folded her arms, glaring at me. I was getting through.

"No one," I repeated. "No one protected me either. Same for Yvonne, once she got out of her unhappy marriage, she had to build herself back up again. And she didn't want you to feel this way, John, she wanted to help you, didn't she? I know the feeling; it was the exact reason I became a police officer, so I could help people."

"She can't help me now. She's dead."

"Do you really want to protect whoever killed her? Do you want your wife and son to drag you down with them, or do you want to tell us the real story of what happened the night Yvonne died?"

"No." He shook his head furiously, startling me.

I thought I had been making progress and that my show of vulnerability might have given John Brandon the strength to stand up to his wife once and for all, and either refute her story or confirm it.

"No?" I stole a glance at Georgiou, still looking as furious as ever.

"He's just like her," John muttered.

"Who is?" I asked. Even Chris looked confused now.

"He's just like his mother," John continued. "Obsessed with people's perception, a temper and a bad attitude. To the church, he's the golden child, the first to volunteer and help out. To his mates, he's the bad guy, the one who makes his dad buy him fags and booze. He had me figured out before he could walk. I can live with Helena and her rage… I can't cope with him."

"Jacob has a violent temper like Helena?" I asked, still uncertain at what John was saying.

He hadn't raised his head again; his eyes were still glued to his trembling hands. Beside him, his solicitor opened her mouth a few times, thinking of things to say, but ultimately, she remained quiet because even she didn't know where this was going. John nodded his head, the movement jerky and robotic.

I leaned in closer. "John. Did Jacob kill Yvonne that night? Did he do it because he thought she was trying to break up your family?"

John Brandon shook his head violently, thrashing side to side like he was having a seizure. "If we're in prison," he mumbled once he'd stopped shaking, "if we're all in prison, I won't have to see them. I won't be trapped."

"John. Did your son murder Yvonne Garrington?"

"We'll be in different prisons, other sides of the country."

"John. Listen to me. Did you help a member of your family cover up Yvonne's murder? Who was it?"

"Helena's just trying to save him, give him a chance at life."

"Who killed her?"

"Jacob. The boy. He did it."

## Chapter Twenty-Four

Jay's cry echoed around us, bouncing off the sea wall to one side and the waves on the other as he resolutely yelled "Fuck off!" to a nearby seagull. The gull scarpered at his shout and retreated to sit with its two friends on top of a groyne, lamenting its failure to steal one of his chips. The tide lapped towards the top, creeping in with a steady pace.

I had sand in my shoes. My chips were cold. But damn it, I loved this.

"Can't remember the last time I had fish and chips," Chris mumbled, sounding happy through his mouthful for what was probably the first time in his life.

"And by the sea as well," Jay said. He threw his head back with delight and the breeze tussled his hair. "We should definitely do this more often."

Next to me, I heard Aaron stifle a laugh at the pure innocent happiness of our co-workers; our friends. We'd walked along the beach from the two-toned cliffs at Old Hunstanton all the way to the sea wall, where the tide was almost in now. Soon we would have to get off the sand and walk back the mile or so we'd travelled, but none of us wanted to be the first one to turn back. Maddie led the group, several steps ahead, still forging on with more energy than the rest of us combined. She'd finished her chips and the wrapper hung out of the pocket of her hoodie. Jay and Chris followed her, both dressed in civvies after a well-deserved day off but neither fussed about sandy socks or seaweed-covered shoes. And Aaron and I were behind, dawdling, not saying much to each other because we didn't need to. We were happy just to walk.

The most surprising thing about our little trip to the seaside the day after we'd arrested the Brandons was that it had been Aaron's idea. I had the feeling he had an ulterior motive, but I couldn't figure it out.

"Oh," I said, catching Aaron's attention, "I couldn't sleep last night so I read that email from Simon Hartley."

"Mmm?" he replied through a mouthful of chips.

"Well, I was right. They want me to give a statement for Sam's upcoming parole board hearing. I said I would, I'm meeting with one of the Victim Support team next week."

"Really?"

I wasn't sure whether to be offended at how surprised Aaron looked but he quickly, and wisely, schooled his expression back to apathy. After a moment to consider this, he gave me a small smile.

"Well done," he said.

Eventually, as the dying sun lit the sky in bright orange and brilliant pink and the sea lapped at Maddie's trainers, she headed up a set of sand-washed stone steps and sat on the edge of the sea wall. Everyone followed.

"This is nice," she remarked, taking in a deep breath. "But seriously, what's this really about? We never hang out like this, unless it's down the pub."

One by one, everyone turned to Aaron, the last to join the group of legs dangling over the sea wall. In just a few short minutes, the tide would be high enough to splash our feet.

He shrugged as he tossed the last scraps from his meal, held in his hands in a paper wrapper, into his mouth. For a moment, I wondered if his reluctance would win out and he would make up some excuse to hide the real reason we were here, but in the end, he spoke as he looked out across the beach. "I need to talk to you all and I thought this would be better discussed somewhere far from Price's reach. At the station or the pub, you can never be sure who's listening."

A ripple of confusion ran through the group. They even looked to me, as if I had some idea of what was going on. I frowned back. I was as clueless as they were. We were alone out here, save for the odd jogger or dog walker. With the tide in and the season finished, there was little in the way of tourists and the locals paid us no attention.

"What do you mean?" I asked Aaron.

With a deep, exhausted sigh, Aaron's gaze drifted to the rippling sea. "I've known Price for years. I've always had my suspicions about the way he works, and I think he knows that. Ever since the Ali Burgess case, he's been pushing harder, digging deeper, trying to find out what I know. We're so disconnected from head office out here on our side of the county. Price runs the police force like a dictator would. At head office, he's surrounded himself with like-minded officers, sycophants and such. I'm worried he'll turn his sights on us next."

"Why would he?" Jay asked, but his face soured as the moment he spoke, he realised the answer to his own question.

"Because," said Aaron, "I know what he's really like. I don't bow down to him like they do. Now he has an inkling about Anna and me, he knows he has some leverage over me. He wants me out."

"Why?" I asked. The more Aaron spoke, the more worried I became. He was able to speak with calm and measured indifference, but in some ways that worried me more; it meant he was hiding something.

"I know something about him."

"What?" asked Chris. He too looked concerned, and it sent an icy shiver through my spine.

Aaron shook his head. "It doesn't matter."

"It does," I replied.

"Fine, but now's not the time for details. The short story is that I worked on an old case with him, years back when I was a DS and seconded to Norwich for a few months. When I uncovered his involvement in it, it all disappeared overnight. He pulled strings, paid people off – I don't know. Anyway, he worked his way up the chain quickly after that and we've avoided each other ever since."

"He's dirty," said Maddie, more matter of fact than anything else, although there was a slight undertone of fear in her voice, as if saying the taboo word had given her a chill.

Aaron gave a stiff nod. "Price makes me run the station at Lynn and I put up with it to keep him off our backs. It works. Well, it did…"

Along the line of the sea wall, I heard Jay snigger. "It worked until Anna started causing problems."

"Hey! I don't cause problems."

"All right, incidents," he conceded. "Basically, Price is pissed because Anna gets herself into trouble and draws attention to us."

"Bingo." Aaron grimaced, and when I shot him a look, he gave me a sheepish one back. "Sorry, Anna, it's true. Over the years, your magnetism for trouble has been containable, but these last few times, I couldn't stop Price finding out. And now he suspects us, he'll be looking for any clue or excuse to get rid of me really. And probably you too."

"Great," I said, sighing with a level of sarcasm only Maddie could best.

When I glanced down the line at them, I realised their expressions all mirrored what I was thinking – what Aaron was saying was concerning, and Chris, Jay and Maddie knew him well enough to see that him telling us meant he was serious.

A sudden movement in the corner of my eye, out at sea, made me jump and I flinched just as Maddie and Jay dived away from the sea wall. A large wave crashed underneath them, covering the rest of us with a spray of salty water. Their quick reactions weren't enough to save them as a shower of seawater rebounded up from the curved seawall, as if chasing them away. They regarded each other, Jay's windswept hair now wet and sticking down the side of his face, and Maddie's hoodie patterned with water droplets. Then they burst into laughter.

Taking our cue, each of us rose to our feet and we started back towards the clifftops at a slow amble. I discarded the rest of my salt-water-covered chips in a litter bin. As we climbed up along the sand-dusted promenade, Maddie pulled her wet hoodie over her head and threw it at Jay to dry his hair off. She turned to Aaron, walking backwards.

"You have nothing to worry about. Your secret is safe with us." She gave him a wink.

"I know," he said, sounding reassured.

Nods of agreement came from Chris and Jay.

"You know," she continued, "that this whole debacle could be avoided if you sling Anna. She's the one that attracts trouble."

They all laughed as Maddie stuck her tongue out at me. She was joking and I knew that; once upon a time, I might have thought she was being serious. Her sense of humour was growing on me. I tried to line up a clever comeback in my mind, but it evaded me when Aaron took my hand, a smile still lingering on his lips.

He squeezed gently. "I know. But as far as trouble goes, she's worth every bit of it."

Together, the five of us set off back along the dusk-covered wall, keeping a wary eye on the raging sea below as it threatened to rise up once again. Aaron pulled me away from the edge, and I gave him a grateful smile; ocean spray blew around us on the breeze and the sun glowed over the Wash as it touched the horizon.

The End

If you enjoyed this book, please let others know by leaving a quick review on Amazon. Also, if you spot anything untoward in the paperback, get in touch. We strive for the best quality and appreciate reader feedback.

editor@thebookfolks.com


www.thebookfolks.com

## Also in this series

**CATFISH (Book 1)**

It is not without some malice that rookie detective Anna McArthur is called "crazy" by her colleagues. She certainly tends to act first and think later. But when Anna discovers the body of a murdered woman who has "catfish" carved into her chest, she feels a personal duty to do everything she can to up her game and find the killer.

*FREE with Kindle Unlimited and available in paperback!*

# Other titles of interest

## LASTING INFLUENCE
### by Linda Hagan

When two social media influencers are kidnapped, DCI Gawn Girvin is called back from extended leave to investigate. One of the abductees is the son of the Norwegian Ambassador, and the powers that be want the matter sorted quickly. Yet Gawn's search for the couple will lead her to places that intersect with her own troubled past.

*FREE with Kindle Unlimited and available in paperback!*

## THE MYSTERY ON THE CORNISH COAST
## by Christine McHaines

Most people relish going to sunny Cornwall. Not so private investigator Quentin Cadbury, who is forced on a fool's errand by a career criminal who has his teeth into him. Tasked with delivering a package on pain of death, the hapless private eye is sent on a wild goose chase. Can he wrong-foot a master villain?

*FREE with Kindle Unlimited and available in paperback!*

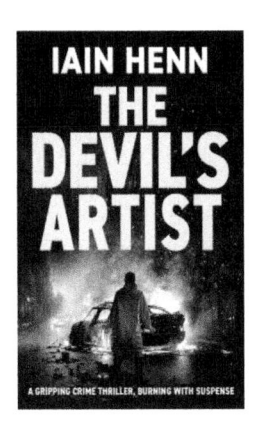

**THE DEVIL'S ARTIST**
by Iain Henn

When a massive wreck on the interstate kills several people, a mural in Seattle that seems to glorify the disaster creates outcry. However, upon discovering that the painting was created days before the event, criminal investigators are baffled. Are they dealing with a psychic artist, or someone who played a role in the incident? Soon other murals appear, and the race is on to stop further tragedy.

*FREE with Kindle Unlimited and available in paperback!*

**THE BOOK FOLKS**

*Sign up to our mailing list to find out about new releases and special offers!*

www.thebookfolks.com

Printed in Great Britain
by Amazon